BATHORY
Memoir of a Countess

A. Mordeaux

Bathory: Memoir of a Countess
Copyright © 2008 A. Mordeaux

BookSurge Publishing
7290 Investment Drive
Charleston, SC 29418

Manufactured in the United States of America

See "Author's Note" at end of story for
pronunciations and further information about the
subject of this book.

ISBN 1-4392-0174-9
Library of Congress Control # (LCCN) 2008931877

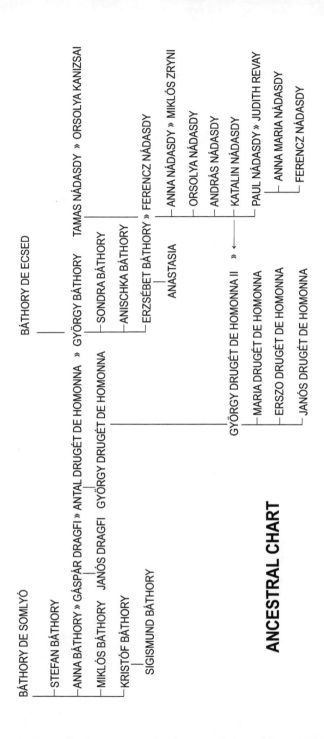

ANCESTRAL CHART

BÁTHORY DE SOMLYÓ

├─ STEFAN BÁTHORY

├─ ANNA BÁTHORY » GÁSPÁR DRAGFI » ANTAL DRUGÉT DE HOMONNA » GYÖRGY BÁTHORY

├─ MIKLÓS BÁTHORY   JANÓS DRAGFI   GYÖRGY DRUGÉT DE HOMONNA

└─ KRISTÓF BÁTHORY

   SIGISMUND BÁTHORY

BÁTHORY DE ECSED

   GYÖRGY BÁTHORY   TAMAS NÁDASDY » ORSOLYA KANIZSAI

├─ SONDRA BÁTHORY

└─ ANISCHKA BÁTHORY

   ERZSÉBET BÁTHORY » FERENCZ NÁDASDY

   ANASTASIA

├─ ANNA NÁDASDY » MIKLÓS ZRYNI

├─ ORSOLYA NÁDASDY

├─ ANDRÁS NÁDASDY

├─ KATALIN NÁDASDY

└─ PAUL NÁDASDY » JUDITH REVAY

GYÖRGY DRUGÉT DE HOMONNA II   »   ←

├─ MARIA DRUGÉT DE HOMONNA

├─ ERSZO DRUGÉT DE HOMONNA

└─ JANÓS DRUGÉT DE HOMONNA

├─ ANNA MARIA NÁDASDY

└─ FERENCZ NÁDASDY

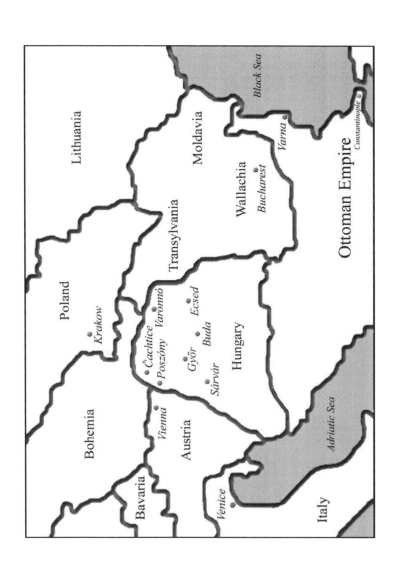

Prologue

armth. Delicious warmth surrounded me. My governess Mira hummed a soft lullaby and rocked me gently as I sat across her lap, drowsy and contented. I inhaled her sweet scent and allowed myself to fall asleep. I was startled awake by screams and shrieks. Mira picked me up and held me tightly as she ran through the castle. She stumbled a bit, but did not release her grip on me. Fireballs were thrown in through the castle windows, lighting brilliant tapestries and furniture afire. Servants ran in all directions to escape. My older sisters, Anischka and Sondra, ran through the hallways from their chambers and caught up with Mira and me, as we searched for a way out to safety.

I could not see my parents, and I prayed that they were safe. As we tried to exit, a burly man whom I did not recognize grabbed Mira's arm and threw her to the ground and started to bludgeon her with a club. I rolled to the side, barely escaping his punishment. Sondra grabbed my hand and we escaped through a window, leaving Mira behind.

A cold wind whipped around us as my sisters and I ran through the grass into the forest of ancient oaks.

Anischka and Sondra followed closely behind me. Out of breath, we scrambled up the branches of one tree, ignoring gravity's pull. As I climbed ahead of my sisters, I looked back and realized that one of the men chasing us had grabbed Anischka's ankle and pulled her down from the tree. Another man grabbed Sondra, and both of my sisters were thrown on the ground.

More men arrived and circled the girls, while others helped pin them down. One took Anischka by her long dark locks and yanked her head back while he fondled her breasts. My view of Sondra was blocked by some tree branches, but I could hear her scream in protest. Someone struck her, and kept striking her until her screams turned to whimpers. I could hear a man laughing, and another moaning. My mind could hardly keep up with the sights and sounds my eyes and ears were processing.

After what seemed like an eternity, my sisters, stripped of their clothing, were taken beneath the oak in which I was perched. I shivered, and the branches scraping my skin felt like death's cold fingers trying to grasp at me. I waited with my eyes shut tight, saying a silent prayer in my mind.

When the men left the forest, there was silence, all but for the noise of rustling leaves in the breeze. I climbed halfway down the tree and when I looked around, I saw that my sisters had been hanged; their exposed bodies were swaying to a lifeless dance led by the wind.

One

The flames of torches flickered around the court of my father, Baron György Báthory de Ecsed. Seated beside my mother Anna Báthory de Somlyó, he was dressed in crimson robes of silken velvet, and his long, dark hair fell around his shoulders in tight ringlets, which he twirled unconsciously with his long, bejeweled fingers. When he stood, his sinewy body moved with grace, and towered over the betrayers of the House of Báthory.

He looked down his long, straight nose and addressed the criminals. "You will be punished severely for the deaths of our daughters and the destruction of our property," he said to the men who attacked our castle, killed my sisters and plundered the local villages. He circled around them as they kneeled. Five were caught by the nobles, and more were being brought in for interrogation.

"You are evicted from your lands and banished from this region. Your wives and children will be brought here and killed in front of you today."

The men were all farmers, and had been responsible for leading a revolt against my father and the other nobles for raising taxes. They had burned buildings and destroyed our vineyards, killed our livestock, and then tortured, raped and killed many of the nobles' children, including my sisters.

I stared at the men, seeing through them as I daydreamed about my ordeal with my sisters. That day, when my uncle Miklós had found me, I was in such shock, he had trouble coaxing me down from the oak tree.

"Come to me, my darling, my sweet child. It is safe, I have you." Bold and bear-like Miklós climbed up through the branches of the great oak and tucked my slender body safely under his arm. He examined my bruises and scrapes, and tried to shield my eyes from the sinister sight of my dead sisters. In a way, they looked like rag dolls hanging there, their faces lifeless. As I studied them, they looked like the dolls my governess used to make and give away. A slight giggle erupted from my lips. Miklós thought I was crying as I turned my face away; I could barely contain my laughter as we made our way back to the castle.

My attention was brought back to court when the prisoners were moved back away from Father's throne to make room for the display to come. My older brother János was seated next to me. He fidgeted with the trim on his doublet. I could tell he was somewhat bored as he watched our father govern the court and administer punishments, although János was no stranger to treachery. He was a cruel, menacing boy, and I avoided him at all costs and made sure that I was never alone with him. When I was much younger, I would fall prey to his experimentations, which were frequently torturous or lewd. Throughout his youth, no small child or animal was safe alone in his presence.

One by one, the families of the men were brought before my father and told to kneel. Some of the men begged for mercy, but their protests fell on deaf ears. The guards brought forward the farmers' children. Their ages ranged all the way from infant to adolescent, most of them were crying, and all of their faces were full of fear.

My father grabbed a blond-haired boy, no more than three years old, and started beating him. The boy's father screamed and begged for mercy. When he tried to get up to charge at my father, the guards pushed and pinned him down to the floor by skewing spears through his arms and legs.

"Please have mercy! Please kill me instead! Let him go, I beseech you—"

The boy's deafening screams filled the room. My father continued to beat him, and did not stop even as blood ran from the child's pale, diminutive face. His battered and bruised little body was motionless when Father stopped beating him.

His father screamed to the deities, "Why? Why? I cannot bear this! Please kill me now. I have no reason left to live!" My father obliged him with his sword.

"My lord, who is to be next?" The guards seemed anxious for more blood.

"Bring me a girl, I care not which."

A beautiful young girl, near my age, was brought to kneel in front of my father. She was very frail, with large brown eyes and long silky auburn hair. I envied that hair. It fell in waves to her slender waist. When she was dead, I thought I might like it for myself.

Moving closer to the girl's parents, he told them, "You will now see what it is like to have your daughter tortured as you did mine." He proceeded to loose the fly of his breeches and forced himself on the young girl. He tore her clothes and pleasured himself like an animal as she cried and tried to fight him off. He slapped and punched her when she fought, and finally, she submitted to his lewdness. The girl's mother whimpered as she was forced to watch. My mother sat in her throne with an uninterested look on her face, as she fanned herself with an ostrich feather fan. János stopped his fidgeting and paid close attention to Father's actions. He smiled as the girl was subdued. When Father was finished with the girl, he instructed the guards to take her to be boiled.

"Wait, Father!" I implored him.

"What is it my daughter?"

"I want her hair. Please, may I have it before she is sent away?"

The girl's mother stood up, "Are you mad? You horrible little girl! That is my daughter's hair. That is my baby, you cannot do this!"

"Yes, my sweet. Guards, sheer her and then be rid of her." My father glared at the woman as he re-laced his breeches. He walked over to her and slapped her so hard, she fell over. He lifted her up and threw her over to a guard.

"I want this woman's mouth sewn shut. I will not listen to this drivel. When she is finished, release her."

The guard took the astonished woman over to a banquet table and tied her to a chair so that she could hardly move. To keep her mouth immobilized, her lips were pried widely apart at the sides of her mouth, and a wedge of leather was placed inside. As the guards held the woman's head, a chambermaid brought a needle and silken thread and began the task of stitching the woman's mouth closed. I admired the chambermaid's fine sutures, even through all of the blood.

I looked back at the girl. The guards grinned at each other as they pushed her down the hallway. "We would like to have our own way with her before she's done." My father motioned them to leave and turned to scrutinize the men's wives who knelt before him.

He grabbed a pregnant woman from the group and dragged her to the center of the court. She raised her arms up to block the beating she expected to receive. Instead of raising his fist to hit her, he kicked her. She doubled over in pain, crying and gasping for breath as the pointed toe of his boot sunk into her swollen belly.

"Please," she implored my father, "please stop for the sake of my baby, ple—" She never finished her pleading. My father slashed her throat with his dagger.

"Bring to me this woman's husband." The gentle looking man had on a stained tunic and grimy breeches. He had been pulled from the fields as he was harvesting grapes. It was questionable as to whether or not he had anything to do with the revolt.

"What is your name?"

"Juri, my lord."

"I shall allow you to live. I banish you from my estates, and you will leave with nothing but the clothes you wear this moment."

Juri looked stunned. He had just lost his lands at harvest time, all of his belongings, and his most prized possession, his pregnant wife.

"Living with these sights in my mind makes me welcome death's scythe." Juri lowered his head and lunged for my father's dagger. He managed to grab a hold of the hilt, and pulled the dagger out of my father's grasp. Juri hesitated. The court guards were all at him, spears and swords ready to lance him to pieces. Father straightened his back and stared into Juri's eyes without fear.

Tears ran down Juri's rough and weathered face. He turned the dagger on himself; the blade sank into his chest, and mingled the blood of his dead wife with his own.

"Bring me a new sword and dagger," my father ordered. "I have many more punishments to deliver," he said, as he looked around at the small crowd of farmers and their families.

He chose a young male, known to be one of the rapists of my sisters. A guard brought him to kneel before the court.

"I've been waiting to see you," Father said, darkly. "Remove your hat in my presence."

The man glared back at him and refused. He folded his arms across his chest in defiance.

"Take off your hat! Take it off now!" Still, there was no response from the insolent man. Father turned to a guard, and whispered a request. The guard left the court, and returned quickly with a small bag.

"You will see where your defiance leads you. If you will not take off your hat in my presence, then I will make sure it stays on your head in your grave." He produced two large rusted nails and mallet from the bag. It took two guards to get the insolent man to kneel, but they managed. With two firm strikes to the first nail, the man's arms were pinned across his chest. With the second nail, the hat was affixed to the man's head. He fell to the ground, arms still crossed, hat affixed.

"Bring me another offender," Father called to the guards. Another alleged rapist, named Benedek, was brought forth to kneel. "You are one of the men responsible for soiling my lovely daughters, are you not?"

"I am. I enjoyed them completely as they fought me

and screamed for their lives!" Benedek snarled back at my father. Spittle dripped from his lips. Father stood back, seemingly unshaken with the man's cruel remarks.

"I see you have no children for me to use as an example for your punishment. May you never bring forth offspring to this earth."

The guards took down the Benedek's breeches and tied a string tightly around his testicles. They held the man still while Father castrated him with his dagger. Benedek screamed in shock and gasped for breath as the guards held him. "You will dine tonight on the sum of your parts. Take him to the infirmary and see to it that he lives—for now."

I was mesmerized by Father's power and all of the blood I had seen that day. My skin tingled with excitement. I was filled with enthusiasm that the people responsible for the deaths of my sisters were punished accordingly. *This should teach these people a lesson to remember,* I thought smugly.

A guard broke my attention as he delivered the hair I had requested. I tied the long beautiful locks with one of my own ribbons from my hair. I sat and watched the rest of Father's court, all the while I ran my fingers down the hair as if it were a lap animal. It was a comfort to feel while I listened to the girl's shrieks as her life was ended.

As we dined that evening, Father made a point to discuss the day's court.

"We should continue to make an example of these savages to the people of the surrounding villages," Father remarked as he sliced into the roasted pheasant and mortresse in front of him. "I think I shall have the guards display some of these examples tomorrow."

"Yes, my dear. That should serve to remind people to respect those in power," my mother said. She always complimented my father after his courts—either for his generosity or his mercilessness.

As I picked at my food, I thought about how no one outwardly mourned my sisters. Everyone was more concerned about the savage farmers and their disobedience to the nobles.

I surveyed my parents as they spoke. Father was dressed in his usual finery of pale blue silk brocade, slashed and jeweled with sapphires, the same color as his large eyes. He moved with grace and ate in a dignified manner. Often, he would sit back in his chair, sip his wine and reflect quietly without venturing into the conversation at the dining table.

Mother was dressed in a bold red Venetian gown, heavily jeweled and embroidered. My mother's servants spent hours readying her for court as well as for dinner. They created many ostentatious hair styles with her brilliant red hair. She changed gowns several times each day, saving the more remarkable imported designs for the evening meal. She was always dressed in colorful garb, which included embroidery, precious gemstones and feathers.

I wondered what Father had seen in her to want to marry her. She had been widowed twice before she married him; she had János with her first husband and another son by her second husband. The circumstances of her late husbands' deaths were never mentioned, but I was sure Mother had something to do with them. The thought made me smirk, which brought disapproving looks my way.

"Erzsébet, mind your manners in our presence!" Mother snapped. I bowed my head in obeisance and they eventually returned to their conversation. A servant girl brought a wash basin for cleansing hands, and then proceeded to drop the basin near Father.

"You stupid vermin!" Father screamed at the girl.

"I beg your forgiveness, Your Excellency." She lowered herself and tried to clean up the mess. Father slapped her hard across the face.

"Be gone from my presence, and send someone else in here to clean up this mess." Father believed servants to be on the lowest level of social hierarchy. He would spit and scream at them, hit, beat, slap, molest and torture them, and did not feel remorseful or guilty afterward. He treated the stable horses better than he did any servant. Mother was even worse, especially to her own chambermaids. I learned how to administer my own servants by watching my parents.

I continued to move my food around on the golden-edged plate. The slices of pheasant meat swam in fat, tangy verjuice and spices. I wondered how the castrated rapist liked his dinner. With morbid curiosity, I asked to be excused and I headed for the infirmary.

As I approached the doorway to the infirmary, I paused to listen.

"By order of His Excellency, you are to consume what is on this plate. Should you refuse, we are instructed to assist you in following through with his orders."

"Rot in hell! Send that plate to your blood-thirsty master!" Benedek was restrained on a bed, but had enough vigor to make me fearful of his escape, so I walked hurriedly down the hallway toward the gardens.

The tranquility of the gardens soothed my frayed nerves; it was a place I visited often when my senses overwhelmed me. I pinched and crushed fragrant herb leaves with my fingers. I inhaled the scents and rubbed the precious oils on my skin. I laced some herbs through my hair and walked toward the orchards.

Summer had ended, and the orchards flaunted their fruits and nuts. The chill in the air became crisper each day, while the daylight shortened. I bristled at the thought of the winter snow that would cover the surrounding landscape.

As I approached the orchard, I could hear some noises from behind a high row of hedges.

"Stop, no more, I can't take you so hard," a girl's voice rose in protest.

"You will take me, and you will show me that you enjoy it. You said you would do anything for me, didn't you? Prove your love for me." I could hear my brother János as he argued with the girl.

"I will try," she whimpered.

I walked around the corner of the hedge and found János and a girl together. She was a frail blonde girl, bent over a large rock, skirts up over her waist, and she looked back at me with surprise. I recognized her as one of my mother's younger servants. She blushed deep crimson and tried to pull her skirts down to cover herself. János pinned her down to the rock and stared back at me blankly.

János did not seem affected by my discovery and did not bother to pull up his breeches from his ankles or even hide his erection. I shifted my gaze from his eyes to his curved, reddened penis and then to the ground in mild embarrassment. I walked quickly back up toward the castle. I could hear János slap the girl and he continued with his savagery, intent to receive his pleasure.

When I reentered the castle, I looked into the

infirmary and saw that Benedek had been fed his meal. He struggled on the bed as he asphyxiated on his own vomit. The guards stood by and watched, happy with their ability to carry out Father's orders.

Two

ire roared in the parlor fireplace of my mother's suite of rooms. Her chambers were always lavish and comfortable, decorated in colorful imported silks and expensive finery. Besides me, the only other people allowed into her rooms were her special servants, her sister Sondra, and my father on the rare occasion she felt lusty enough to invite him. I inhaled the sweet scent of lavender; there were dozens of fresh bouquets all around the rooms. They were my mother's favorite flowers and Father made sure the servants placed them wherever she might be in the castle to sweeten her tempestuous moods.

As I worked silken threads through my needlework, I half-listened to my mother and Aunt Sondra discuss some boring business about our home, Castle Ecsed. As she and my mother clucked about like hens, I rose from my work to stretch my legs.

"Stop, Erzsébet! Stop this instant!" My mother grabbed my satin skirts from behind. They were soaked through with blood. My mother scared me a bit with her shrillness. She pulled my skirts from my body and examined the scarlet blood stains. It looked like an animal had been slaughtered on the shiny fabric.

"Nika, bring Erzsébet another set of skirts and some rags immediately!" The chambermaid arrived quickly with my new garment and quietly instructed me on the use of the rags.

After I was composed, and settled with a warm drink, my mother and Aunt Sondra approached me.

"Erzsébet, you are now the only daughter we have left. Your duties to the family have changed with the arrival of your menses and we feel now it is time to prepare you for marriage." Sondra nodded her head with every word. My mother walked across the room to retrieve the accounts of my dowry.

"You must marry Baron Ferencz Nádasdy. We have made an alliance with his family, and we feel it will be a suitable partnership. He will be made one of the richest men in the empire, and our family will be lords of vast lands of this realm. Your betrothal will be two years. We will expect your behavior over this time to be exemplary and that you will not shame our family name, and that you will be deserving of your station."

It was done. I had no say in the matter, nor had I ever laid eyes upon the man I was supposed to marry. There was no celebration of womanhood, no motherly advice on the monthly "curses" or womanly talk as I might have had with my sisters. I was just a trading piece. Mother must have read the look on my face.

"I will have no arguments from you, Erzsébet. This is what must be done to secure our family's wealth and status within the emperor's eyes."

"Yes, Mother. I will submit to honor our family." My eyes were downcast and I did not mean a word of what I said. I told Mother what she wished to hear in order to placate her and be excused from her presence.

"Good. I will start planning the wedding ceremony and feast with your future mother-in-law. You are excused." She waved me away and I left quickly.

I made my way to my suite of rooms and shut the heavy wooden doors behind me. I climbed onto my soft bed, surrounded by luxurious silks and satins. I stared up at my billowy canopy of curtains, and wished I was elsewhere. I had felt ill and cramped most of the morning, but my mother's plans made me feel worse. I pulled the curtains shut and cried myself to sleep.

After five miserable days of bleeding and listening to my mother and aunt plan my future, I left Castle Ecsed for a walk. I took the path through the woods to visit my dead sisters. I picked bunches of the season's last wildflowers along the way, and looked forward to my visit. The family crypt always made me feel safe; I liked to explore all of the hiding spaces within and examine the remains of long-dead relatives. Their bones and decayed bodies fascinated me. Since my sisters' deaths, I enjoyed curling up next to their decaying bodies to nap the afternoon away.

Even though my sisters could not speak to me, I would tell them of happenings around the castle. Sometimes, I thought could hear their whispers of secrets and sisterly gossip to me. As I laced some of the flowers through their hair, I was proud to tell them of our father's valiant punishments delivered upon their assailants.

"Dear sisters, your deaths have been avenged. Father's court was magnificent as he delivered punishments to the men who killed you," I said as I wrapped the flower stems into an intricate pattern in Sondra's beautiful hair. "I am to be married to Ferencz Nádasdy. I do not look forward to this arrangement."

Sondra answered me, *Erzsébet, you fool! He would*

have been my husband had I not died. What luxury and riches you will know if you marry that man!

Anischka chimed in, *Yes, yes, and all the riches and lands imaginable. Take him as your husband and be sure to please him. You will reap the benefits for years to come.*

I considered what I thought I had heard my sisters tell me; still I was sad about my impending marriage. I left the crypt and walked to Danijel's cottage. Danijel was the son of a wine merchant, and he was being trained to run his family's business. His mother had died when he was an infant and we had been close friends for as long as I could remember. We had started to become more than friends to one another.

"What is wrong, my darling?" Danijel knew something was amiss the moment he saw me, and his impish grin faded. I looked deeply into his eyes, and I wanted to swim in the green lake-like pools, away from my life.

"I am to be married. Now that my sisters are dead, I have no choice. The House of Báthory will be joined with Nádasdy."

"Oh my sweet," he held me tightly, "we must hide our love and not speak of our meetings to anyone." He stroked my long hair, and kissed my cheeks and forehead. He drew shut the heavy drapes of the cottage and lit some candles. I inhaled the sweet scent of bees wax as they flickered in the darkness of the room.

"I agree we should keep this a secret, but will there ever be a future for us? We cannot always hide, and I will not be happy in silence and secret for all of our days."

"We will run away and I will marry you. We will live together forever." His kisses grew more passionate, and the urgency of our future melted away. His mouth tasted sweet from the freshly harvested grapes that were on the table. I was weak with anticipation. We had gone as far as kissing and petting, but we always stopped short of making love. This day was different, as if we were both desperate to fulfill an urgent need.

The lacings of my bodice and corset were undone easily by his skilled fingers. My skirts dropped to the floor, and my silk chemise sailed over my head as he pulled it from my body. He sat and regarded me for a moment.

"You are the most beautiful girl I have ever seen." I blushed, and tried to push aside the thought that he had seen other girls. He went on, "Your skin is so perfect, like a baby's." He ran his hands up and down my body, and generated a buzz of heat between us. I parted my lips to say something, but my words evaporated.

I did not know how to undress a man, and even though I had seen acts of sex, I had no clue what was about to happen or the feelings I was about to experience.

Danijel's body felt fluid with my own. He helped me take his clothing from his body, slowly, one piece at a time. He sat on his bed and pulled me onto his lap, into his warmth, and I soaked in how safe he felt. His kisses trailed up and down my neck, between my breasts, all the while his hands roamed the rest of me.

I felt an urgency to be one with him; to be a part of his energy. He gently tugged at my ear lobes with his teeth and tongue. I felt like a hungry animal. I wanted to chew at him, tear at his flesh and make it my own. I explored his body with my hands and tongue and bit his nipples a bit too fiercely.

He enjoyed the vigor of it all, and effortlessly

plunged into me. It was like a jolt of energy went tearing through my body. The pain of his entry into my virginity, coupled with the pleasure and heat from our love drove me insane. I ran my fingers through his sandy halo of curls and over his sinewy body.

He finished quickly, and lay back to rest. As he caressed me, he leaned over and smiled at me, his eyes full of love. I inhaled the scents of our coupling and I wanted more.

"You do not know this pleasure yet. I must show you what this passion is all about." He gently cleaned me and then caressed me up and down my thighs and between my legs. Easily he brought me to the peak of pleasure. He was ready to enter me again, and as he did so, I felt like I was pushed over the edge of eternity. I wanted to be in that cloud of pleasure forever. In a snap it was gone.

"Again! Again!" I demanded.

He laughed at me and held me close, "Wait my sweet, wait, you can keep going, but some people can only reach that point once for each coupling."

"Then we will keep doing it. I want it more. Now I know what this drive people have for lovemaking is all about." We made love several more times throughout that afternoon, and I was able to reach that cloud of pleasure each time. Danijel was exhausted, but was happy to indulge me.

Sore, but sated, I left his cottage in the woods, and the surreal comfort of his home, to return to the reality of my life.

I found that by counting the days between my monthly bleedings, I could predict when to use the rags given to me by the chambermaids. Each month, I was doubled over in pain from cramping, and I kept to myself most of the time. I did not feel like to deal with my relatives, and could only bear so much of my father's court.

Five months after my betrothal, I realized that the number of days since I had bled was near sixty. My thoughts raced. *Where was it? When would it start again?* I kept the rags handy, just in case, but I still felt all of the monthly symptoms. Perplexed, I went to Nika, my chambermaid, and asked her what could be wrong.

"Oh my dear, for two months you have not bled?" She seemed shocked when I told her. "Let me look at your breasts." She loosened my bodice and corset, and then pulled them off, more coldly than Danijel had done. She felt around my sore nipples, and pointed out that they looked to be a shade or two darker than normal.

"What's wrong with me Nika?"

"I think you're with child, my dear." She felt my bloated abdomen, and then told me to put on my chemise while she went to get my mother.

A few minutes later, my mother burst through the doors of my bedroom with Aunt Sondra in tow. She looked as though she had been interrupted while the maids were dressing her hair. Her rusty-colored tresses were only half-pinned into place, while the rest was left unruly.

"Who is the male responsible for this atrocity?" My mother was beyond angry. Her voice shrilled and her hands trembled, and her large brown eyes were even larger than usual with a wild look about them.

"Danijel and I have been together. We wish to be married—"

"Danijel Norsko? The wine merchant's son? He is the nephew of one of the men that killed your sisters!

How could you even want to be with him?" She twirled around the room, her velvet skirts billowed. Sondra sat down, unable to stand steadily through the ordeal.

"This cannot be happening. You were to be married into the House of Nádasdy. You are an embarrassment to us all. Orsolya will be most displeased. The shame of it all!" Orsolya was my future mother-in-law, who in accordance with my mother and Aunt Sondra, planned the marriage.

"Mother, I—"

"Do not speak! I will not have you speak at all. You will not breathe a word of this to anyone. We must cover this up and never speak of it. You will be sequestered to bear this shame and we will send it away after its birth." Mother and Sondra left the room. I was in tears as I sat on the edge of my bed.

My right arm went numb, and my head felt as if it were in a fog. Saliva dripped from my mouth and I could not swallow it down, or bring my hand to wipe it away. My heart felt as if it would race out of my chest. I fell backward onto my bed and fainted.

I awoke in a fog. Nika stood over me, her face was full of concern. My thirst seemed unquenchable, and I felt great pain in my head. It would be the first of many times that I would be gripped by a falling sickness my apothecaries called Saint John's Evil.

After three days in my chambers to myself, I emerged to face my family. My mother told only Orsolya about my pregnancy, and I was to live with her until the baby was delivered. I was outraged. I would never be able to see Danijel again, and I was forbidden to leave the castle grounds without an escort. No argument would deter my mother from her decision.

I retreated to my chambers, and spent most of my hours reading a book Father had given me about Greek mythology. It felt like a solemn escape from my troubles.

One evening, I managed to slip away unnoticed, and I went directly to Danijel's cottage. I had no cares about the brisk chill in the air as I trudged through the remaining snow and slush of the receding winter.

"Where have you been, my love? I have been so worried about you. I thought about coming to see you at the castle."

"Oh, Danijel, never do that. My mother would be furious. I must tell you something. I am with child and I will never be able to see you again. My mother is sending me to Sárvár to give birth."

"No! No, this cannot be! I cannot live without you! And you are having my child?" He placed his hand over my abdomen, and caressed me.

"Yes, it is true and when the child is born, it will be sent away. My heart aches. There is nothing I can do. I am sorry, my love."

"But our baby? What will happen to it? I want our baby, I want us to be a family..." His voice trailed off and I had no answers for him.

I started to sob and he held me tightly. "I am sorry. I must get back to the castle before they discover I am missing. I am not allowed out without a guard. I wanted to tell you so that you did not worry about me. I love you for all time." I brushed my fingers lightly across his full lips.

"Don't go—no, this cannot mean the end of us."

"It has to be. I have no other choice." With that, I turned and left. My cries of anguish on the path home rivaled those of the mountain wolves whose howls were carried across the valley by the icy wind.

When I returned to my chambers, my mother and aunt were waiting for me. They did not seem concerned as to my whereabouts, nor did they comment on my swollen eyes or tear-stained face.

"We have some special herbs from the apothecary. They are supposed to rid you of this child. You will drink the tea we made for you and wait in your chambers until we see that it has worked." Mother handed me the hot cup of herbal tea. As I drank the acidic-tasting beverage, it warmed me and I thought about the possibility that the herbs might work. Even though I was torn in wanting Danijel's child, I knew that giving birth to it would mean that I would be sent away, never to see him again.

"We will check on you in the morning. Do not leave the premises," Mother said. Silently, Aunt Sondra gathered up the small cloth bag of leftover herbs and followed my mother out of the room.

I slept fitfully that night. Voices and phantoms tormented me in my dreams. Danijel's sorrowful face appeared, his hands outreached for me across a dark and foggy river. I recognized it as the River Styx from my book of mythology, and he was on the side of the living. I could see that he was shouting, but I could not hear him. I tried to wade across the river, but souls of the dead reached up and grabbed at my legs. I awoke with a jolt, shivering.

The herbs made me sweat profusely, and I had to change my bed clothes twice that night. By the time the sun peered into my room like an unwelcome stranger, I had started to cramp and bleed. When I arose, my bed linens looked like a murder had taken place. Perhaps my child was dead within me, and there *had* been a murder of sorts? I could only hope that the herbs would work.

Three

I bled for four days, but my symptoms of motherhood persisted. My mother ordered Aunt Sondra to take me into the village under disguise to visit a midwife. The midwife was a portly old woman with a kind face and sweet voice. She did not ask probing questions, but she knew I was not married. She confirmed I was still with child.

When I returned home, my mother knew from the look on my face that I was still with child. "You can't be! We used the herbs as they instructed us. This is Satan's spawn, of that I am sure. If I could rip it from your body with my own hands, I would!" Mother unleashed her fury as she ripped a painting off of my bedroom wall. It sailed across the room, and landed in front of the door. A servant came in to check the cause of the noise and when she saw my mother's face, she bowed her head and left quickly with the painting.

"You are to go to live with Orsolya immediately. I will have the servants ready some of your things and you will stay with her until this whole ordeal is finished."

"Mother, who will take my child?" I knew I risked

worsening her anger, but I had to know.

"I will give it away to some lowly peasant family in another kingdom. I do not want it ruining our opportunity for your future marriage."

"But—"

"Enough! I will not argue these things with you. For all we know and can hope, the child will be stillborn." She turned and left my room, Aunt Sondra followed behind her.

Spring had arrived, but I hardly noticed. I packed a few things to take with me on my voyage to my future mother-in-law's home, Castle Sárvár. I knew very little about Orsolya, and from what I had been told, I didn't think I would enjoy living with her. She was an extremely shrewd, autocratic, religious, middle-aged woman, and I had overheard my servants talk about her coldness and how she had raised such a fierce fighter as her son grew to be. My heart was filled with dread, not only because of my pending imprisonment with Orsolya, but for what I was learning about my future husband.

It took many days to journey across a rough and curvy path to Sárvár, which did not agree with my morning sickness. I emptied my stomach many times along the way. It was a miserable trip, and knowing that I would never see Danijel again, or possibly even hold my own child, made my heart ache.

Every bump and every turn made my head spin, and it was all I could do to keep myself from screaming. My silk gown was stained with my own vomit, and my face was crusty with dried tears.

The carriage only stopped a few times each day, briefly for the driver to attend to the horses, and also to set up camp for the night. My physical and emotional misery prevented me from enjoying the beautiful spring flowers and awakening countryside.

Castle Sárvár, a grand, pentagonal-shaped stronghold, appeared on the horizon, bold and monolithic. The grounds were vast and well manicured. The evening shadows coupled with the castle's austere appearance frightened me. In a sense, this place would be my prison; I would not be allowed to emerge until the following summer. I had lost Danijel, my freedom, and my child.

I exited the carriage and waited to be escorted up the front steps of the castle. I counted the stars as I stood, and ignored the frigid cold. I wondered if Danijel thought of me. I hated my mother for sending me away. I wanted to escape and return home to murder her. *Oh, there were so many different ways a person could die,* I thought, and I knew I could devise the perfect death for her.

The huge doors of the castle's front entrance creaked open, and my acrimonious feelings for my mother would have to be set aside. A small young woman, about sixteen, stepped forward to greet me. She wore an unornamented black velvet gown and a simple black hood over her blonde hair. Her soft voice and diminutive presence contrasted with the vastness of the castle.

"Greetings, Lady Báthory. We are pleased to accommodate you in our home. I am Katalin, and I will see you to your quarters. My mistress shall summon you soon."

I did not address her, nor did she give me the chance. She turned and led me through a maze of dark hallways, sparsely lit by torch fire. The floors were highly polished alabaster stone, inlaid with onyx in an intricate pattern. The Nádasdy coat of arms hung proudly in the foyer of the castle and was emblazoned everywhere one looked. The walls were adorned with centuries-old paintings that hung alongside brilliant religious medieval tapestries. The paneled walls were ornate with gold-leafed moldings. I was led up a grand staircase, bordered by cherubs and satyrs, whose smiles appeared to mock my situation.

Finally, we arrived to my rooms. They were warm, well lit, and comfortably furnished. I inhaled the scent of sandalwood and beeswax when I entered, and immediately explored the space. I did not notice Katalin had locked the doors on her exit, but it didn't surprise me when I tried to open them later.

My bed was decorated with fine pink fabrics and plush coverlets. Nearby were a Turkish divan and two ornate chairs. A desk was positioned near the window, along with a large selection of books. I ran my fingers over the soft leather covers, and admired the gold leafing and tedious calligraphy as I flipped through them. My father had paid a high price for tutors to teach me to read and write, and I fully intended to take advantage of the books during my imprisonment.

I heard the sound of a key work open the lock on my doors. They opened to reveal a middle-aged woman with a grim look on her face.

"I am Orsolya, your future mother-in-law. I am to be your guardian during your time of pregnancy. You are not to leave this suite of rooms without my consent or escort. You will not have visitors during your stay, except for the midwives. You will be expected to attend classes with your tutors while you are here, read the Bible throughout your day, and abide by my rules without hesitation. Should you break any of the rules, you will be punished accordingly."

Orsolya walked around me as she spoke. She stopped directly in front of me and regarded my vomit-stained gown. I met her gaze as she looked into my eyes. She didn't expect to see the defiance, the strength of my will.

"I see you have a disobedient streak. I gather that's probably what led you into this condition. This is God's way of punishing you, and you will feel His full wrath when you deliver this child. Pain is an excellent teacher." Her pewter-gray eyes matched the tone of her satin gown and gray hair.

"I will call upon you early in the morning for scripture reading before we break our fast." She locked the doors as she left. I was glad to be rid of her, and I was anxious to strip off my clothing and sleep. I was so tired from the voyage, the pregnancy, the anguish, that I fell into a deep sleep as soon as I got into bed.

My days with Orsolya were filled with lessons in etiquette and manners, as well as her recitals of Biblical verses and stories of pious women of the Bible. She was a devout follower of Martin Luther. In addition, Orsolya thought I should learn about the business of administering the castle. Orsolya was an astute businesswoman and knew precisely how to manage the Nádasdy's numerous estates. She brought in tutors to further the education my father had started, including teaching me more languages and music. Eventually, I would assume her position in the household, and I needed to be prepared to run things in the likely event that Ferencz was away on military business.

I thought of my future husband, Ferencz. He would add my name to his own and we would be Count and Countess Báthory-Nádasdy. I scrawled his name, and then our names together on parchment, and admired how they looked linked with one another.

After a few months, Orsolya grew to trust me and allowed me to wander about the castle on my own. As I explored the huge castle, I admired the portraits in the hallways. There was a portrait of a man that I would spend a great deal of time observing, sometimes for hours if my swollen feet and legs would allow it. I was mesmerized by this man—he had thick shoulder-length dark hair, chiseled facial features, and beguiling dark eyes. He was dressed in rich a golden brocade zupan with a fur-lined mantle over one shoulder. His eyes implored me to look; I could not pass the portrait without paying homage. I would visit the portrait everyday without fail and stare into the man's eyes.

"I see you've found Ferencz." I did not realize Orsolya was behind me as I stared at the handsome face in the painting. "He was eighteen when we commissioned that painting. Such a beautiful boy, he always was."

"Yes, he has beguiling eyes."

"They'll tell you stories of his fierceness when you hear people speak of him. They even call him the Dark Lord when he fights. He has the Nádasdy spirit." She admired his portrait and I felt a common bond with her as we stood together.

"What was his father like?"

"Tamas? Just the same as his son. A skilled fighter, beloved as well as feared by many. Tamas was a great promoter of education, and he built a school in Uj-Sziget, and was also responsible for creating this," she said proudly as she handed me a beautifully printed Bible, a product of the castle presses. "He became Palatine, second only in rank to the emperor. Unfortunately, we lost Tamas in battle. Ferencz was only seven." She sounded mournful as she spoke of her late husband's demise.

"Ferencz chose to be a military man very early in life, and has become an admirable fighter for our country, and was decorated with high ranking titles early in his career. The emperor speaks very highly of him. Ferencz used to love listening to his steward in childhood tell him the tales of King Árpád, the first Hungarian King, and also stories about the fearsome Prince Vlad Tepes," she said, wistfully.

I would not get to meet Ferencz until after my child was born and taken away. He knew nothing of my predicament. As I looked as his portrait, I felt embarrassed by my pregnancy. *Why should he want me?* I thought.

Each day, I grew larger and more tired. Most days, after Bible study, I stayed in my room and studied the wonderful library of books available to me. My baby would kick and turn. As I pressed my hands over my swollen belly, I thought of how my love for Danijel had faded with time. I thought I would feel love for him forever, but even the rage and resentment for my mother had faded over the months.

I grew restless and bored of my environment, and I took no interest in sewing or any of Orsolya's tutoring. The summer heat reminded me that the time of my child's birth was approaching quickly, and Orsolya had the midwives instruct me as to what I would experience during the birth. Their instruction did not fully prepare me for the experience.

I hated being pregnant. I was ready to rid my body of my symbiont, and to hear Orsolya speak of the child made me feel like I was going to give birth to Satan himself. I felt bulky and swollen, and I outgrew my most beautiful garb; it was replaced by dark, dull-toned linen gored tunics and simple surcoats.

I toiled away the hours learning German, Greek,

Latin, and mathematics. I read whatever I could wrap my mind around, including philosophy and theology. I grew distasteful of the Bible, as it was a daily chore that Orsolya insisted I read and recite. My mind seemed to argue with each passage, but I knew better than to voice my opinions to Orsolya.

In the bowels of the castle, there were many storage rooms and dungeons. I found a large stash of decaying books in what looked like an abandoned library. Orsolya instructed me never to explore this part of the castle, but the order only piqued my curiosity and rebelliousness. I stole away to read as many books as I could, and found fascinating subjects such as astrology, medicine, and paganism. The works of the Devil! I had found a wealth of information!

One sultry afternoon, I lay across a bench with my feet up, entertained by a book about astrology. I felt a strong pain sear across my back and I panicked. *What if I started giving birth while reading these books?* I was not going to allow that to happen. Orsolya's punishments would be too much to bear.

The pains in my back worsened and I forced myself to climb the creaky stairs. As I opened the door of my book vault, I doubled over in pain and knew labor had most definitely begun its course. Suddenly, I felt a gush of fluid run down my legs, but I continued my climb up the stairs. I crawled back to my chambers, and managed to climb onto my bed.

As the coming hours unfolded and the day passed into night, the pain intensified. My maidservants called for the midwives and Orsolya. They all stood around and watched me writhe in pain.

"Leave me be! Get out!" I screamed so loud, the gatekeepers across the castle moat likely heard me. One of the midwives tried to subdue me, but I didn't want anyone to touch me. I scratched and kicked her away, and she stood back from the bed.

Orsolya grabbed me by the shoulders and shook me. "Erzsébet! You must get a hold of yourself. You must listen to the midwives and breathe properly. Your pain will be lessened if you do as they say." She looked into my eyes and wiped away the sweat from my forehead. I nodded in agreement and let them help me.

Hour by hour, each wave of pain washed over me, and tore through my body; it clenched me to the depths of my soul. If I cried, the pain worsened. Once my breathing was under control, I noticed the pains were coming more quickly and I had an overwhelming desire to bear down. My body was ready to be rid of this child and I gladly obliged as I pushed it out.

"Push, Erzsébet! You must push this child into the world with all of your might!" Orsolya yelled. Sweat dripped from my hair. It was so hot in the room I could barely tolerate it.

My child's head crowned, and I pushed harder, against the stinging pain. Before I knew it, my baby had been placed across my belly. Orsolya helped clean her as one of the midwives cleared the child's mouth and throat. She let loose a lusty wail, and squirmed around on me as she cried.

I observed my daughter after the umbilical cord had been cut, and I felt somewhat repulsed by her appearance. Orsolya noticed my reaction. She wrapped the girl tightly in a blanket and went to sit in a chair by the window. The midwives cleaned up the afterbirth and helped me change into a clean chemise. My maidservants washed my hair and skin with cool, rose scented water.

"You may name your child if you wish, but you will

not be allowed much time with her. Her new parents are on their way to receive her," Orsolya said.

"I didn't think that would happen so soon..."

"It is best this way." She handed me the child, who seemed content to sleep, swaddled tightly in her blanket. I had thought about several names, both for a boy and a girl, but each time I settled on a name, I wondered what was the use?

"Anastasia," I declared. I had found the name in a book I had found in my book vault. It meant *rebirth*. In a sense, we would both be reborn into new lives.

I lay back in my bed and slept. A day later, I awoke in tears as I grasped for my child. My breasts ached and were full of milk. I cursed myself for letting Anastasia go. *Why didn't I steal the child back and run home to Danijel? Why couldn't I have resisted my mother and Orsolya?*

For days, I refused food and drank little. I felt as if my child had died—better she had than to be taken from me. Orsolya checked on me often, but did not interfere with my mood. My maidservants worked to keep me clean and presentable, but when I chose gowns, I chose from Orsolya's plain kirtles. Even though I was happy to be relieved of my burden of pregnancy, I had no joy in my heart, and did not feel like caring for my appearance.

The falling sickness returned with a vengeance. The worst fit overtook me in the gardens one morning. I went out to try and enjoy the last of the summer sun and my limbs began to tingle. A gardener saw me fall to the ground and came to my aid. My body jerked and twisted as I lay in the grass. He called more servants over, and one placed a wedge of leather in my mouth. I do not remember the entire fit, but they told me that I nearly bit off my tongue and one of the gardener's fingers. When I came to, I was in my bed; my head pulsed with a seething headache. I could still taste the leather that had been placed in my mouth.

I was plagued with many more episodes through the winter months. Orsolya prayed over me, the apothecaries gave me many herbal brews and poultices, and bled me with leeches, but nothing would rid me of my fits.

A few weeks later when I felt recovered, Orsolya summoned me from my chambers.

"It is time for us to make wedding plans now that this debacle of your pregnancy is over. I have sent word to your mother and she will be visiting us soon."

"I have no desire to be a part of these plans."

"Do not act with such defiance!" She slapped me across my face, nearly knocking me backward. "You will do as you are told." She paused and regarded me for a moment. "If it will mend your heart, I will convey to you a brief report of your daughter."

"Yes, may I hear of her?" My face stung and I could still feel the impact of her slap across my cheek, but my heart leapt at the chance to know about my child's fate.

"She is with the wine merchant's family, with her own kin."

"Danijel?"

Orsolya nodded. "His aunt and father came for her."

Finally, I felt a sense of relief that my child was safe with her father.

Four

y wedding day was planned for late springtime at Castle Varonnó, nestled between the Carpathian Mountains and the High Tatras. A warm zephyr blew through the castle gardens, and coaxed the flowers and trees into colorful glorious bloom, which contrasted sharply with the dark stones of the enormous ancient castle.

Over four thousand dignitaries and royalty had been invited from all over Europe, and arrived over the weeks prior to the ceremony. The Holy Roman Emperor Maximilian had been sent an invitation, but had declined due to illness, although he sent his son, Prince Rudolf in his stead. My mother's brother, King Stefan of Poland, made the voyage from Krakow to attend the wedding, and also to discuss military business with Ferencz.

Orsolya and my mother argued fiercely about my wedding gown. Orsolya thought I should be dressed in virginal white gilded in gold, while my mother held tightly to the notion that my gown should be blue. My seamstresses made several gowns and none of them suited the matriarchy.

"You have no sense of fashion, Orsolya. You have

been locked away in your castle with your dusty Bibles for far too many years to have any idea what my lovely daughter should wear on her wedding day." Mother glared at Orsolya and would not back down.

"Should she be adorned as a Jezebel for her wedding day, Anna?" Orsolya countered.

I interrupted their argument. "Dear mothers, please do not argue over my most sacred clothing. I will choose the gown of my liking and you will not be displeased, and neither will be our treasured Ferencz." Surprisingly, they were both placated by my maturity and request.

I chose rich emerald green silk velvet, which contrasted beautifully with my auburn hair. The seamstresses worked countless hours on the acanthus embroidery, which was sewn in golden thread, magnificently trimming the edges of the gown. Amid the leaves and acorn scrollwork were clusters of pearls, emeralds and diamonds. My coronet was a heavy golden circlet given to me by my father, and had belonged to his mother. He had his jeweler work in pearls, emeralds and diamonds to match my gown.

My maidservants took special care in bathing me the morning of the ceremony. Goat's milk, special herbs and honey were added to a warm bath drawn for me. Nika scrubbed my body and massaged oil into my skin.

"We must take special care of your lovely skin, my lady." I hadn't noticed until that moment that I paid little attention to my looks, although I had been told they were an asset I should never ignore.

"Do you think that I am beautiful, Nika?"

"Oh yes, very much so, my lady. Your beauty will capture the hearts of many."

"There is only one that I wish to ensnare in the

matters of the heart. Ferencz is the only one that matters."

"No, my lady. Your beauty and your youth should be treasured. From your skin, to your hair, to your well-shaped body, your beauty is your prize, not only in the matters of the heart, but also in the matters of getting what you want in life."

After I thought about her statement, I understood and considered a more rigorous beauty regimen.

Ferencz did not know that I was already intimately familiar with his home Sárvár, although Orsolya, through an exchange of letters, had told him about me. I looked forward to being the mistress of our mansions, even though Orsolya would still be living at Sárvár. Ferencz would be away on military campaigns at the emperor's whim. Already my mother was planning my social engagements. While my hair was being prepared, I overheard her as she discussed plans for my attendance at many family and political events.

It took nearly an hour for my hair to be adorned with golden leaves and tight ringlet curls. Another hour was spent securing my underpinnings and the wedding gown. I slipped my feet into soft leather shoes, and felt quite a bit heavier decorated in my garb. When Orsolya and Mother saw me for the first time, they both gasped and ran to me like two giddy girls.

Once my makeup was complete and every detail of my clothing was checked, I was taken by carriage across the castle grounds to the church for the ceremony. The church was filled with the aroma of incense and the music of harps, lutes, and vielles. Colors and fragrances of imported exotic flowers adorned the entire church.

Nobles of the Báthory and Nádasdy families sat

at the head of the church, dressed in their most ostentatious finery. King Stefan and Prince Rudolf sat next to my mother. A hush fell over the crowd as my father escorted me to the pulpit, where waiting, was a priest and alongside him, stood the most handsome man I had ever seen. The beguiling eyes I had spent hours studying while locked away at Sárvár stared back across at me with intense interest. I shivered with excitement when he flashed a pleased smile at me. All eyes were upon us at this first meeting.

The priest droned on in Latin, as he asked God to bless our marriage and shower us with prosperity. I did not pay close attention to the words of our ceremony, although I was fluent in Latin. All I could do was stare at Ferencz, and think of what life would be like alongside him. He was a beautiful creature to behold. He had piercing dark brown eyes and a full head of dark wavy hair. His face was free of the scars of war and he had a neatly trimmed mustache. He was broad shouldered, much taller than me, with the muscular physique of a skilled warrior. He wore a dark green zupan adorned with the same acanthus embroidery as my wedding gown. At his hip, a brilliant szabla hung in decoration, and his tall boots shone black. I was mesmerized, and hardly noticed when I was asked to speak my vows.

His gaze searched my soul as he peered into my eyes. We were mutually besotted with one another. The world was blocked out and time stopped as he raised my gauzy veil to kiss me. I was lost in that kiss and I longed for more of his soft, hungry lips. After the ceremony, Ferencz took my hand as we were presented to our families and guests.

The reception began and we sat at the high table with other high ranking nobles. Ferencz spoke in a clear baritone voice, and was eloquent in speech. He could hold a conversation of the simplest nature as well as argue the most complex subjects with educated expertise.

We danced, dined and drank with much merriment for many hours after the wedding. Musicians and acrobats entertained all. Everyone enjoyed the free-flowing wine and lavish foods my mother and Orsolya had chosen. Thousands of animals were slaughtered and prepared for the wedding and the weeks prior in order to accommodate the guests and their retinues until the ceremony; pheasant, duck, fish, oxen and lamb were cooked to perfection in delicious sauces and herbs. The freshest spices, vegetables and exotic fruits were imported and made into soups, stews and pastries. Perfectly aged cheese and figs were served with clover and orange honey to compliment the mead, wine and ale.

As we dined, Ferencz would lean over and feed me tenderly. I savored each bite he delivered—I would have eaten anything he had fed me as I was still under the spell of fresh infatuation.

"I will take special care of you for all time," he whispered to me.

"And I you, my husband. Dance with me," I smiled at him and he took my hand and led me to dance. He was athletic and did not tire easily. I felt weightless as he lifted me and twirled me around.

Finally, the evening came to a close and our parents bade us good evening before we were shown to our marriage bed.

"May you be blessed with an abundance of happiness and wealth, my child." Father kissed my forehead and caressed my back as he held me. He was a sight to behold, dressed in his finest court garb of crimson silk brocade, studded with diamonds. His garb rivaled Mother's flesh colored gown, which had been embroidered with flowers and encrusted with pearls.

"Thank you, Father, for this most wondrous day. You and Mother were most generous and gracious," I humbly thanked my parents for their expense and labors over my wedding.

Mother held me tightly and whispered, "See that you please your husband well tonight and bring forth many legitimate grandchildren for me to spoil!" She squeezed my arm and stepped back next to my father. I blushed.

Even János dispensed well wishes to us, which surprised me. "Dear sister, much happiness to you and my new brother." He bowed to us and stepped back behind our parents.

Orsolya paid her well wishes to us before she went to her suite of rooms. I could see that she loved to stay at our Castle Varonnó. Mother had Orsolya's chambers lavishly decorated and stocked with fragrant flowers and herbs.

Ferencz led me to our bedchambers which joined our two suites of rooms. A large four poster bed of heavy dark mahogany, carved with angels and cherubs, stood waiting. It was decorated with plump coverlets and pillows, and a decanter of wine sat by the bedside. A fresh bouquet of lavender rested at the head of the bed. I picked up the bouquet and inhaled the sweet scent. Ferencz took the herbs from me and held me in his arms.

I drank in his warmth, and held him tightly. He ran his fingers through my hair, and gently released it from its ornamentation. He was gentler than any of my servants had ever been in undressing my hair.

"You are a beautiful creature. I will teach you many things," he promised. I felt guilty that I had already known a man—Danijel—before our marriage. Mother warned me that Ferencz could reject me if he found that I was not a virgin bride. The men of our time, especially warriors like Ferencz, believed the pureness of their brides to be of the utmost importance, and that they should have first pluck.

"I will be sure to learn from you, dear husband, and I hope that I please you."

"Do not worry. Your very existence pleases me."

He loosened my clothing and it fell to the floor. I allowed him to undress himself, not wanting to seem too forward and knowledgeable. He joined me on the bed as we regarded each other.

I felt no shame in gazing at him. Ferencz was fine-looking in every way. His powerfully built body was lithe and taut. Each muscle was defined and made him look like a perfectly chiseled statue. His body hair contrasted dark to his pale skin, and though it was sparse, it was soft and comforting as I lay my cheek against his chest.

His hands explored my body, and he rubbed me vigorously into a desperate heat. My tongue found his nipples and he groaned with excitement as I licked and bit each one.

"Ah, you do what comes naturally. Yes, that is good..." He was in ecstasy as I continued to lick his body. He still assumed I was an inexperienced virgin.

He grabbed a handful of my hair and pulled my head back, to expose my neck. He devoured my skin with his kisses and bites, licking me up and down my neck and around my ear lobes, pleasuring me in equal as I had done him.

He was inflamed. The hardness of his erection

poked my skin as he moved over me. I longed for the pleasure of it, but I waited patiently.

Ferencz was surprised when he entered me, "You are not in tact."

I waited for a moment before I responded by thrusting my hips into his. We moved with heated synergy together, and for many hours we were as one.

I fell asleep in his arms, warm and safe. When I awoke, he was already dressed and smiled as he stood over me.

"Wake up, my beauty."

"Such a sight you are to behold in the morning, my husband," I smiled at him, and pulled the sheets up around me.

"I enjoyed you last night, and I look forward to many years with you. I must prepare our sheets for our relatives' benefit." He sat on the edge of the bed and pulled out his dagger.

I sat up quickly and he placed his hand gently on my leg. "No, no, don't worry, I would never hurt you," he slit his finger and allowed a few drops of blood to soil the sheets.

I relaxed and felt appreciative of his thoughtfulness. He saved us both from the embarrassment of my past indiscretions. I took his finger in my mouth and suckled the blood until the cut clotted. I took in another finger, and then another. His clothes were off again and he was back in bed with me.

"You are insatiable," he lamented in jest, though I knew he was happy to gratify me, yet again.

It was mid morning before we broke our fast. The servants brought us a platter of cheese, soft bread and honey. We both devoured the food like hungry beggars.

Afterwards, my maids dressed me and I joined Ferencz in the gardens.

Behind some tall hedges, just as I had caught him before, I heard my brother's voice behind the leaves. This time, a young boy protested. I blushed and did not want Ferencz to see what I knew my brother had been doing.

"We must go visit the orchards, they are in lovely bloom right now." I tried to pull Ferencz away from the hedges, but he heard the boy's objection to whatever János was doing to him.

"No, I must go see if someone is in trouble, wait here." He walked around the hedge and towered over my brother and the boy. I ran around the hedge and saw that János had a stable boy bent over a rock in the same manner he'd had the servant girl the prior fall at Ecsed. Apparently, this was his favorite way to entertain his lewd urges.

"Are you here against your will, young boy?" Ferencz asked, while glaring at János.

The boy looked back at Ferencz. János did not bother to release him or cover himself. "No sire, I am here in my own pleasure." The boy blushed.

"Leave us be, Erzsébet, unless you fancy watching," János snarled at me.

Ferencz walked over and slapped János across the face with the back of his hand. The jewels in Ferencz's rings tore into János's flesh. "You will never raise your voice to my wife in disrespect again. Should I hear of it, I will avenge the deed myself, expeditiously."

János finally pulled up his hose and dried the blood on his face with his cloak. "Welcome to our family, *dear brother*," János said with a sneer and he turned to leave. The boy had collected his clothing and was already gone.

"János had best hope that I do not cross his path again."

"Not to worry, he is scheduled to leave to be married in Wallachia soon. Come, my darling, let's salvage and enjoy the remainder of our time here. I banish the thoughts and visions of János from our minds." I waved my hand around as if to drive away a demon.

"Thank you, Erzsébet, I want to enjoy what is left of our time together. I shall be taking my leave of you once we reach Sárvár."

"Oh, but why so soon, can't you stay with me but for a little longer?" I pleaded.

"The emperor has plans for a new military campaign against the loathsome Turks. Even though it tears my soul to be away from you, I must go. I must protect my status within the army. Ever since the announcement of our betrothal, there have been numerous political strategies aimed at removing me from my rank. I think there are many jealous men who covet my position and new wealth."

"Will you be away long?" I felt my lower lip quiver, but I held my emotions in check, as I did not want to cry in front of Ferencz.

"One never knows with military duty; the emperor is a capricious soul and I am directed at his will. I shall return to you, and while I am away, you hold my heart." He placed my hand over his heart as he looked into my eyes.

I savored my time with Ferencz before he left. Each night on our journey to Sárvár, his garrison set up a special tent for us to share alone and away from the rest of the entourage.

We brought Orsolya with us on the voyage, and

even though she enjoyed her stay at Varonnó, she longed to be at her own home, tended by her own servants. Orsolya was delighted when I reported that Ferencz was pleased with me. Mother had her worried that Ferencz might send me away after he found out that I was not a virgin.

Once we reached Sárvár, Ferencz spent one more night with me before he left for his tour of duty against the Turks. I noticed that each night I spent with Ferencz, his lovemaking grew more forceful. His forcefulness excited me, and I looked forward to learning more of what pleased him.

When I awoke the morning after Ferencz's departure, I overheard some servants as they whispered about him. They readied my clothing for the morning, and stood in my wardrobe as they shared their gossip. They were new to me, installed at Sárvár since I had left to be married. I was not fond of any of these girls, and I longed for my former servants. I would remedy that as soon as I could. I needed people that could be trusted, not those who would speak of my husband so distastefully.

"You know, I have heard Lord Ferencz is quite the ladies' man when he's away on military campaign."

"Shh, you mustn't speak too loudly or she will hear you."

"I wonder if he has to pay for his whores or if they line up at his tent once they hear of his penchant for pleasure?" The girls snickered as they gossiped.

My temper flared and my pulse quickened. I charged in and interrupted their loose talk. With full force, I slapped them across their faces. The older one, the one who spoke of Ferencz's whores, fell backward from the force of my blow and landed in the hot coals of the fireplace. Her skirts did not catch aflame, but her hands were burned from the embers that remained.

"That will be *His Excellency* to you and you will not speak of me or my husband in such a manner ever again! You will know my fury frequently should you remain in employment here." The two girls ran out of my chambers and I never saw either of them at Sárvár again.

I took their words to heart as I sat alone in my chambers, staring out into the gardens. *Did Ferencz really satiate his carnal needs with whores?* I felt a pang of jealousy run through me and then I quickly dismissed it. *He couldn't be expected to remain faithful for the many months—even years—that he was to be away, could he? Soldiers must have some outlet,* I thought to myself. I reflected about the differences between men and women. A woman was expected to be trustworthy while her husband was away. Her needs must be met by self-gratification, and only in secret. János certainly didn't subdue his carnal urges, as I'd often caught him as he pleasured himself alone or with other willing or unwilling subjects.

It wasn't fair, and I did not like the idea of being chaste for so many months. *Maybe I should find another man to satisfy my urges*, I thought. I knew that if I found a way to satisfy my own urges with other men, that I must be totally and completely circumspect lest I risk the penalties and shame of broken marriage vows.

Five

ven though the castle grounds bustled with hundreds of servants as they performed their everyday duties, I felt completely alone. I requested my servants from Ecsed, but it would be several weeks before they arrived. I allowed only two chambermaids in my presence. Katalin, the servant of Orsolya, whom I'd met when I first arrived at Sárvár, gladly accepted my offer of employment when she learned of my marriage to Ferencz. The other chambermaid, named Darvulia, was sent from King Stefan's household in Poland as a wedding gift. Her mother, known to be an immediate relative of Prince Vlad Tepes, had been my mother's and Stefan's governess.

I rarely saw Katalin except for in the morning when she assisted me with my routine of dressing. Katalin spent time each morning gently brushing and plaiting my hair into complicated braids, all the while, clucking away softly about the current fashions in England and France. Katalin was also responsible for maintaining my wardrobe, which grew larger by the year. I refused to wear the dull robes and gowns Orsolya favored, and I had many gowns shipped from Castle Ecsed.

Most of my gowns were jewel-toned, and were always encrusted in precious gemstones and embroidery, which Orsolya did not hesitate to call garish.

Darvulia was responsible for my evening routine of undressing and massaging my feet. She also drew warm baths and brought me precious oils and herbs to enhance my skin or hair. I was impressed with Darvulia's knowledge of herbs and medicine. She always knew how to manage my falling sickness, and cared well for me after a fit. I grew to love her and I found myself confiding in her. I showed her my secret crypt of books under the castle, where we would spend hours together discussing astrology and alchemy.

"You should come away with me to celebrate Strinennia, my lady," she said one day as we were discussing paganism.

"Strinennia? Where do you go to celebrate?"

"Not far. One of the head stablemen's cousins is well trained in the occult. She is part of a woodland coven. They meet at each sabbat."

"Orsolya would wet herself if she knew that I had gone to a pagan ritual," I snickered. The thought of her reaction was delicious.

"So you'll come with me, then?" Darvulia knew me all too well.

"Of course."

After my personal servants arrived, I felt more uplifted. Darvulia kept me company and watched over me protectively. We weren't far apart in age; I would be sixteen that summer and Darvulia was twenty-three. Many nights, after she finished my undressing and evening routine, she would climb into bed with me, and we would stay awake, talking and laughing.

One night after I had my evening bath and we had extinguished the candles, she turned to me and ran her fingers through my hair. At first, I took it as a loving gesture of a close friend, but then I felt her lips gently kiss mine. Surprised but curious, I allowed her to continue.

She licked my lips with her tongue ever so lightly and I parted them to permit her kiss to go further. Her kisses were softer than Ferencz's, though just as hungry. She tangled her fingers in my hair a bit tighter and caressed my breast with her other hand. My tongue was engaged with hers in a passionate dance. Her lips left mine and she explored my body with her tongue and hands. Her smooth, svelte body felt cool against my own. Blissfully, she pleasured me, and brought me to the pinnacle of delight many times. She used her fingers with experience—teasing, massaging, tantalizing.

Night after night, until Ferencz's return, Darvulia and I spent together in ecstasy. One night, she brought a carved ivory phallus to bed. It was quite large and well-formed. She ran its cold head up and down my leg and made me wet with anticipation. She plunged the phallus into me and covered my mouth with a possessive kiss.

"Do you miss Ferencz, my dear?" she whispered in my ear. She moved the phallus in and out, and she rubbed all the right spots.

"Not at the moment," I said weakly. I was breathless.

I fingered the pale pink nipples of her full breasts, flicking at their hardness. Her breasts were so round and perfect. I suckled them and my fingers roamed her body. I took the phallus from her and teased her with it. I licked her body up and down, and sank the ivory into her as I licked her clitoris. She reached her climax quickly, as she bucked against my mouth.

Satiated, we both lay in bed, legs intertwined. Moonlight beamed through the window, casting light and shadows across the bed. Was it possible to love two people—a man as well as a woman? I pondered the question silently for a while, and when I looked over at Darvulia I noticed that she had fallen asleep.

I regarded her beautiful body as it lay on top of the silk sheets, her full lips slightly parted as she breathed, and her glorious dark hair spread over the pillow. Yes, I loved Darvulia, but not in the same way as Ferencz. I could still taste her when I drowsily turned over and asked the gods of sleep to take me away.

In the springtime of the following year, we planned our trip to the forest to celebrate Strinennia. Darvulia and I sat in my parlor as we talked about what we should bring for the trip. I summoned the head stableman, whose cousin was the pagan priestess leading the ritual. He had been sent over from my father's retinue. His name was Ján, but many people called him Ficko. He had several deformities of the face and body which I forced myself to overlook. His back was severely hunched, and his face was pitted with the scars of the black plague. He spoke with a slur and had the mentality of a child—an evil child. Even with his deformities, he managed the stables well without much assistance from the other stablemen, and I assigned him many other duties.

"Will you be attending this celebration with us, Ficko?"

"Yes, Your Excellency. I am most honored."

"Wonderful. Please have the carriage ready for our

departure in two hours."

"Yes, Your Excellency," he bowed his already hunched back and left the parlor.

I turned to Darvulia and crinkled my nose. "He's quite ugly, isn't he?"

"Yes, but he is a loyal servant, of that I am sure."

Darvulia had one of the seamstresses make a special robe of velvet for me for the celebration. We took very little with us, even though we planned to be away for several days. Darvulia packed herbs, oils, and candles, as well as a hand-made book of spells she called her Book of Shadows. My curiosity was piqued, so I looked through it when she left the room to go pack more of her things.

The first passage was a short prayer to the deities, thanking them for life, love and light. I flipped through the thick pages and kept reading. The next section included directions and specific uses for herbs and potions. I recognized one of the comforting teas she had made for me after I'd had a fit from my falling sickness.

The book entertained me and I read on and paused at a Latin passage that struck me as intriguing.

Malo a nos libera sed tentationem in inducas nos ne et nostris debitoribus dimittimus nos et Sicut nostra debita nobis dimitte et hodie nobis da cotidianum nostrum Panem terra in et caelo in sicut Tua voluntas fiat Tuum Regnum adveniat Tuum Nomen sanctificetur caelis in es qui noster Pater

I reread the passage and realized that it was the Lord's Prayer in reverse. Just then, Darvulia returned.

"Can you explain to me why one would recite the Lord's Prayer in reverse?"

"It's part of an old ritual of ridding yourself of an enemy. Follow me."

I nodded and followed her to her bedroom, where she had an altar set up next to her bed. She formed a waxen effigy of one of the chambermaids we both detested and we retrieved some hair from the girl's hairbrush. Darvulia melded the hair into the effigy and lit her altar candles. She moved to the center of the room and raised an athame into the air.

"I call forth the elements, Earth, Wind, Fire, Water, and Spirit. Let this circle be cast for power from the Goddess, and protection from our enemies."

Darvulia went to her altar and sunk the athame into the effigy of the chambermaid.

"Cast this person into flame, be it now by her name, Danika, so mote it be." Darvulia focused for several moments on the effigy, and she whispered the girl's name over and over again, along with the chant. She then recited the Lord's Prayer, reversed. I was surprised that she knew the Latin in reverse as it fell from her lips so easily.

Darvulia folded the broken and punctured effigy with the athame into a black silken cloth and she locked it away in a cedar box atop of the altar. She recited more verse to end the ritual and sat with me on the edge of her bed.

"What did the ritual accomplish?"

"In three days' time, or possibly before we return from our trip, Danika will be dead."

I was doubtful, but curious of the outcome.

"We should get going, Ficko will wonder what's keeping us," she reminded me.

The servants had taken our bags to the carriage,

which waited in front of the castle for our departure. We rode for several hours away from Sárvár, along the edge of the Rába River.

A recent rain had brought forth the scent of fresh earth. There was a cacophony of animal sounds intermingling within the lush vegetation. Wildflowers of every sort swayed in the light breeze. Flashes of orange and white poppies, brilliant green carpets of moss and yellow phlox covered the rocks that led to the banks of the raging rapids of the river below.

When we reached our final destination, a woman named Dorotta greeted us.

"Welcome, Your Excellency," she greeted me and curtsied. "Please feel comfortable to join our circle today. We hope that you will find much enlightenment during this celebration of Strinennia." She was a large woman, weighing probably twice what I weighed. She was also very hairy. I noticed her arms were covered in a dark fuzz of hair, and it reminded me of Ferencz. Her long dark hair cascaded down her back, and she wore a black velvet robe. She wore no shoes and no ornamentation.

I walked with Darvulia, Ficko and Dorotta to a clearing within the forest. Large and colorful canvas tents had been erected around a brazier. Closer to the edge of the forest, an area for the ritual had been prepared.

"You may feel free to bathe in my tent and then enter this ritual skyclad or with a robe," she said back to our group. I didn't understand at the time what skyclad meant. Darvulia helped bathe me clean which was something I welcomed after the long trip. I dressed in my newly-made robe and joined the ritual. I enjoyed the silky feeling of the rich fabric against my freshened skin.

We walked into a circle of eight other people, both men and women; they stood in a special formation. I was startled to see some of them were nude. Darvulia leaned over to me and whispered, "Skyclad," and winked at me. There were torches lit to symbolize the four elements and directions. Incense burned in a large cauldron, sending up unfamiliar scents into the air. A small altar was set up and stocked with the tools of the craft, such as candles, crystals, a large leather-bound book, and bowls of herbs and oils.

Dorotta dropped her robe and stepped into the middle of our group. Decorated only by a wreath of flowers in her hair, she raised a giant sword, larger than any I had seen Ferencz carry. With breathtaking power, she wielded the sword over her head and pointed it in the directions of the elements as she recited the ritual in a bold and lusty voice.

"Breath of our Goddess, blow. Be the wind in our sails and spark our intellect and wonder.

Passion of our Goddess, empower us! Touch us with your breath of passion and place flame in our souls.

Flowing Waters, blood of our Goddess, move freely and quench our thirst! Your life force pulses through us.

Sacred body of our Goddess, be our strength. Your fertile body nurtures the seeds of life.

From the sapphire sky to the fruitful earth below,

From the fire's flame rises as a tower,

From the flowing water's path and hollow,

Our spirits call, our voices sing of elemental power.

Our circle is cast, and we are between the worlds of heaven and fire.

Direct us, Goddess, to our earthly desire.

By the earth that is Her body, the air that is Her breath, by the fire of Her soul, and the waters of Her living womb, may the God and Goddess reunite."

Four others in the circle had specific duties during the ritual, such as lighting ceremonial candles and adding herbs and handmade bird effigies to the burning cauldron. Dorotta invoked many names of gods I did not recognize. After the ritual was over, we dined together under the shade of the forest trees.

The meal was quite an impressive spread before us; there were fresh figs and grapes, bread and cheese, roasted vegetables and venison, and free flowing wine.

"Will you be setting up an encampment in the forest this evening, Your Excellency?" Dorotta asked as she plucked some grapes from a bowl.

"We did bring supplies for a short stay, but I had planned on going back to Sárvár if daylight permits."

"Feel welcome to stay with our group tonight should you decide to reserve your strength for the trip tomorrow."

Darvulia squeezed my knee and I knew she wanted to stay longer.

"Very well, we should like your company this evening. Ficko, please make ready our encampment after our meal."

"Yes, Your Excellency."

Daylight faded into night, and Dorotta spent most of her time with Darvulia and me, as we discussed the workings of spells and incantations around our campfire. I hungered for as much knowledge as I could absorb; I was fascinated with the power that Dorotta wielded.

"Spells work through your own personal power. The manifestation of your desires is pushed forth by the universe as you summon the elements. It may be used for good or for evil, and whatever energy you send out into the universe will return to you, threefold," she explained. Darvulia and I looked at each other.

We conversed until late into the evening. My head felt fuzzy from all of the wine I drank, and I knew I needed to rest. I looked over at the others in the group and noticed that they were all engaged in sexual acts with one another. I watched for several minutes before Dorotta interrupted my thoughts.

"Care to join us this evening, ladies?"

"Oh, may we, my lady?" Darvulia pleaded with me as a child would ask their mother for a treat.

I hesitated for a moment but answered, "I see no reason why we cannot. I should like to experiment a bit." Arm in arm, we walked over to join the group. We helped each other undress, and I was immediately guided down to the ground and found myself seated on a man's penis. He fondled and licked my breasts as I rode him. He was an ugly man with dark blond hair and rough skin, but well endowed and he knew how to pleasure a woman in many ways.

A woman came over to our tryst and squatted over the man's face, and allowed him to please her with his tongue. I reached around her and massaged her breasts and she moaned and threw her head back to rest on me. Once our threesome was spent, I was moved toward another man.

He was tall and dark skinned with dark curly hair. His demeanor was emotionless and his mood showed no pleasure. He resisted me when I tried to touch him, and he made me kneel down in front of him; my station in life was not important or even common knowledge within this assembly. His full erection was in my face and he guided it into my mouth. I was taken aback a bit by his forcefulness, but I allowed the experience to happen.

After several minutes of pleasuring the man, he

grabbed my hair a bit forcefully and nearly choked me as he climaxed into my mouth. The head of his penis was large and red. He thrust his hips, and sank his penis deeper, nestling my face into his overabundance of hair.

I needed a rest after the dark man, and as I sat back from the group, I watched the rest fornicate before my eyes. Once Darvulia was free, she brought me her scarf to wash my face and a drink of wine to clean my mouth.

"Ferencz should be so generous," I joked.

"I hope that you are enjoying this experience."

"I am, I was just... I have never taken a man in such a way before."

She laughed lightly, "There are many other ways that will also surprise you."

"I'm sure there are. I think I will watch for a while and then go to bed."

"Are you feeling unwell, my lady?"

"No, I just have some concerns about pregnancy. I let the first man spend his seed inside of me. I don't ever want to be pregnant again, nor do I wish to shame Ferencz," I explained to her.

"Don't worry, we have herbs to remedy any chance of that. I will make something for you in the morning."

"Very well, I appreciate your help, Darvulia."

"Are you sure that you are well enough for me to leave you?" I nodded and she went back to the group to intermingle with other men and women.

I watched until I could take in no more and went to my cot and fell fast asleep, with thoughts of my next visit with Ferencz on my mind.

When I awoke, Darvulia had a warm brew of herbs and black tea ready for me to drink. We didn't speak that morning, and my only words were to Ficko to ready the carriage for our departure.

Ficko's disfigurement did not dissuade any of the women the night before. He appeared happy and rested. I wished my experience had been more enlightening.

I was happy to see Sárvár appear on the horizon. As we approached, a body was carried out of the castle. When we arrived and the carriage stopped, I immediately got out and went over to the men who carried the corpse.

"Show this person's face to me and tell me what happened."

One of the men lifted back the shroud. Eyes open, lips parted, Danika the chambermaid was dead. Her head was at a strange angle.

"She fell down the stairs and broke her neck, Your Excellency. Her relatives are here to claim her body."

I looked over at Darvulia and as we walked into the castle, she whispered, "The spell worked." I was stunned but impressed.

Upon settling in after my trip to the forest, a new maidservant assisted me with undressing and bathing. Her name was Minika. I could tell she was young, probably twelve or thirteen, and very inexperienced as an attendant. She poured my bath in a sloppy manner, dripping water all over the floor around the golden tub. I did not like her from the moment I met her, and her rough handling of me made me hate her. While undressing me, she ripped my gown, and let my corset drop to the wet floor, which showed a great lack of respect. While taking my hair down from its complicated dressings, she pulled it several times.

"Must you be so rough?" I snapped at her.

"Sorry, my lady." Her eyes lowered, although I

could see no penitence, and she continued to be a brute.

I reached over and lifted her chin up so that I could peer into her eyes. Anger boiled inside of me, and I unleashed it with a hardy slap across her smug, pale face. Her cheek bore the red imprint of my hand.

"Be gone from my presence!"

I decided to bathe myself rather than to call for another maidservant. I enjoyed the peace and privacy and stayed in the water until it grew cold. After I dried myself and wrapped a dressing robe around my body, I called for Darvulia.

"Bring Minika back to me, I wish to speak with her."

Darvulia brought back Minika within minutes. The girl did not have the respect for my station to curtsy.

"Down on your knees you little wench. You will show respect for me in my presence."

Minika knelt before me and seemed displeased that she was called back in front of me.

"From what castle do you come? I have never seen you here before today."

"I was brought here by Mistress Orsolya. I am engaged to the nephew of her laundress. I have never attended prior to my employment here."

"You must learn respect for me if you are to continue your service. I am the Countess Erzsébet Báthory, mistress of this house. You are to address me in the proper manner." Minika had no reply and she averted her gaze out the window behind me.

Her petulance irritated me more. I could feel my blood pressure rise, my heart beat faster, and the color rise to my face. Darvulia looked worried, but before she could speak, I struck Minika across the face again, opposite from the first strike. She stumbled back onto her bottom, and caressed her wounded face. I pulled out a wooden switch from my wardrobe and beat the girl, slashing and whipping her pale skin until it bled. The more I hit the girl, the happier I felt.

When I finished beating Minika, she was curled into a tight ball on the floor, sobbing; and still showed no respect for me. Darvulia stood by, assessing the situation.

"Your Excellency, may I suggest a treatment for this disrespectful girl?"

"Please do so, Darvulia."

"Perhaps she needs to be shown the little room in the east tower, the one beneath your library," she said with a coy smile. I understood what she meant, and I agreed that it would be the perfect lesson for the girl, if she lived.

Darvulia stripped the girl's clothing and dragged her by her long, brown hair down the stairs from my bedroom in the west tower, to the east tower basement room. I followed behind as Minika shrieked and kicked at Darvulia the entire way around the pentagonal shape of the castle.

I grabbed a torch from the wall and scorched her skin. "Shut up you little hag!"

Darvulia flung open the door and pushed Minika into the dark, dank void of a room. The girl screamed as she felt the pestilence come alive in the room upon her entry. There were beetles of many varieties, spiders, bats, and rats that dwelled in the east tower room. It was an old storage area, no longer used or maintained. The room had one small portal of a broken window. Its ceiling was high, perfect for the resident bats, which flew around in the dark as the door opened.

No where to sit, the naked girl crouched in the void as she whimpered a prayer. Darvulia slammed the door shut and locked it. An evil laugh escaped her lips and I laughed with her. My spirits were lifted as we walked arm in arm back to my suite of rooms.

After five days, Minika's shrieks, cries and calls for help subsided. I had instructed Darvulia to see that the other servants did not interfere and that girl was fed, but I knew that the pestilence would challenge her for the food. When I checked on her the sixth day, she lay on the floor, insects covered her body. I could see bites on her pale skin, and rats swarmed over the remains of her food.

"Darvulia, please see that this girl is removed from the castle immediately."

"Yes, my lady. Where shall we send her?"

"Out to the forest, I care not where."

"It shall be done." Darvulia turned and left to retrieve Ficko.

Six

had many preparations to oversee before Ferencz's arrival home from his tour of duty. As mistress of the manor, I was responsible for making sure he had everything he wanted during his break from war, and I also managed all of the estate's affairs in his absence. There were twelve major castles and thirty minor residences that required direct management, including Sárvár and Čachtice. Every day, I oversaw and surveilled the granary levels, ordered textiles, organized hunting trips, decided on which animals I wanted slaughtered for the castle meals, reconciled the taxes and rents owed from the surrounding villages, and tracked loans to support the king's war campaigns. I delegated some tasks, but watched everything. Each time we moved the household to another estate, preparations needed to be made to ready our destination castle and as well as implement plans to clear out the castle from which we were departing. Our retinue would visit Čachtice soon, and I needed to delegate staff, food, furniture and other household items to be shipped and ready before our arrival.

Sárvár Castle and its grounds had been readied

in anticipation of Ferencz's return. The gilded walls and ceilings had been dusted, furniture polished, rushes changed, surfaces cleaned. The gardens looked pristine and were manicured with great precision. Not that Ferencz would have ever noticed, but it was done out of respect for the master of the castle.

I was working at the dining table, papers spread, account books towering in a huge stack beside me, when I heard heavy boot steps approaching from the main entrance. I looked up to see Ferencz, in all his handsomeness, come through the doors, his dark red cloak swirled around him. He threw off his hat and his cloak, and they landed on the alabaster floor for the servants to retrieve. His eyes were set on me, and he nearly knocked Darvulia out of the way as he approached me with open arms.

"My love, my heart, I am so enthralled by your beauty." Ferencz knelt and kissed my hand. I blushed with delight.

"I missed you so, I hope to please you so well that you will never want to leave again." I smiled at him and brought him up in front of me, and he proceeded to kiss me deeply, his coarse hands caressed my cheeks as he held my face. He was so grand to look upon; his dark hair had grown longer, his muscles thicker and stronger, and his skin was darker and rougher than I had known it to be before he left.

"I have no doubt of that. Shall we dine?" We walked hand in hand to the dinner hall and enjoyed a grand feast in honor of his arrival. His personal entourage joined us late into the evening. I longed for everyone to leave, so that I might have Ferencz to myself. It had been so long since we had seen one another, over a year had passed. I thought of our first night together often, and longed for his touch.

"Dance!" I heard someone say loudly, and the music went from light and entertaining to festive and overbearing. Ferencz took my hand and we jumped into a fast paced folk dance. People swung side to side, laughing and gesturing as they moved up the line and back, changing partners.

I danced with Ferencz three dances and then retreated to my chambers. I did not feel well, and had not been well all day. Darvulia saw that I had left and she followed me to my chambers.

"Are you unwell, my lady?"

"No, I do not feel well, I think a fit might be—" I fell to my knees, and from there, I blacked out.

When I awoke, Darvulia was cleaning me. During my fit, I had lost control of my bowels, and had soiled my gown.

"You are an angel," I whispered to her.

"I am your loyal servant and friend. I will always be there for you."

I lay back and let her take care of me. I was so tired; I could barely raise a hand to motion for a drink. My body felt like dead weight, and my senses felt confused. I had a strange smell in my nostrils that I could not place, and a salty taste in my mouth. The muscles in my legs were sore, and my head felt like it was spinning.

"Here, drink this." Darvulia helped me sit up and held the cup as I drank. I could not taste the warm liquid, but it soothed me nonetheless.

"Ferencz's first eve back, and I am in this state," I said, feeling deflated.

"Not to worry. I think his entourage will be getting him so drunk he'll pass out before he makes it up to bed. You have plenty of time to recuperate."

Darvulia was right, Ferencz passed out downstairs

with several of his garrison. She called for the apothecary to visit me.

Zoran, the apothecary, arrived at my bedside before I broke my fast with the day's first meal. He listened to my heart, my breathing, took samples of urine, saliva and my hair.

"Your episode was different this time from others, was it not?"

"Yes, it was. I don't remember the fit, everything went black."

"Hmm, yes, I see. Tell me, did you have an unusual taste in your mouth?"

"Yes, I did, I always have that."

"I may have my assistant visit you with the leeches soon."

"Why must people who are sick be bled? I really do not see that it does any good."

"Ah, blood is the life force that races through your veins. It keeps you alive and well. When sick, the bad must be cycled out."

"Since blood is so precious inside the body, does that make it equally so outside of one's body?"

"Yes, there are many valuable uses for healthy blood, different potions for youth and various drinks made to strengthen the ailing."

I considered what he told me and intended to remember to research blood and its uses more in the future.

"When I went to Poszóny to consult with my mentors, I discussed your fits with them. They call these episodes of yours *epilepsija*. It is a disorder of the brain." He pointed to his head as he observed my reaction.

"Something is wrong with my head?"

"In a sense, yes. There is no surgery to fix this

ailment, but we must be vigilant about your care. I will leave some herbs to soothe you, and some instructions for your servants about your dietary needs."

"Thank you, I am grateful for your visit today."

"I will return to check on you, Your Excellency," he said, humbly. He bowed a deep bow and left the room.

Ferencz ate a small meal with me late that afternoon. I felt better, and did not mention my illness to him. He was in high spirits and I did not want to ruin his mood with worry.

"Last night was magnificent. Thank you for planning such a wonderful homecoming, my troops and I enjoyed it."

"It is my pleasure to see that you are happy, my love."

"How have things been for you, are all of the estates running smoothly?"

"Yes, I have had no trouble in managing things in your absence. I have left the accounts for your review, staff lists, inventories, to be read at your leisure, my lord."

"Thank you, darling. I rest well knowing that you are here in charge. Have there been any problems with the servants?"

I thought of Minika briefly, but shook my head and smiled at him.

"Good. I am off to visit with my mother. I shall see you this evening in our chambers, will I not?"

"Yes, I will be there waiting for you, my love."

I walked the halls of the castle, and felt safer since Ferencz had returned. I didn't fear when he was gone, but things felt more right when he was in residence.

As I walked, I thought I heard someone crying. I walked farther down the hall, nearer to Orsolya's chambers in the north wing of the castle. A shout stopped me in my tracks.

"You will obey! Kneel!" Ferencz's voice was raised in rage.

"Yes, my lord! Please, do not hit me!"

I heard the slap of skin and a crash after.

"Pain is a wonderful educator, Iliyan. Learn from me!" I heard another loud crashing sound and then silence. I crept up to the door and peeked in. I saw Ferencz's back to the door. He was looking down at his manservant, Iliyan. He had beaten the boy so badly his face was bloody and his clothes torn.

"Put your hand on the table. Do it now!" The boy obeyed the order. Ferencz, tongs in hand, took a coin from the fireplace kettle and he placed it in the boy's palm. The boy screamed in agony as Ferencz held the boy's hand shut over the hot coin.

"You will learn never to steal from me."

"I am sorry, master, please forgive this transgression. I promise I will be your obedient servant."

I could smell the boy's burning flesh. Ferencz hit the boy again, so hard he fell back against a chair. Not wanting to be caught listening, I kept walking down the hallway toward my chambers to ready myself for Ferencz later that evening.

Darvulia took great care in dressing me for the evening. Katalin helped wash and dress my hair. Darvulia massaged my shoulders and pulse points with the oil of cypress. I selected a pair of ruby earrings and a bold ruby necklace. She selected a loose fitting ruby colored silk robe and dressed me tenderly.

"I wish it were my night to be with you. You look lovely." She embraced me and inhaled my scent.

"Thank you for taking such good care of me. I love you, my friend."

Darvulia finished packing away my toiletries and she left quietly after lighting some sweet-scented candles. Ferencz arrived shortly afterward, dressed in his blue velvet robes. He wore a gold earring in one lobe, and neglected to shave the light velvety stubble from his beautiful face. He held out his arms to welcome me into an embrace, which I drank up greedily.

"I've caught you. You are mine for the night," I said. I didn't want to let him go.

"Yes, I am yours always. Come, join me on the bed."

He took his time undressing me, smelling me, licking my skin. "I could eat you for my dinner." His teeth sank lightly into the skin of my neck. I felt a tingle run through me. His lovemaking was primitive that night, like an animal's heated lust. I enjoyed every moment. He bit me more hungrily over the rest of my body and left marks on my skin, which I admired the following day.

He was a hungry, starved wolf when he looked at me. I was taken aback a bit, but then I wanted to be consumed. He mounted me so roughly I moaned in pain. My moans made him ride me harder, grab my hair tighter. It was delightfully torturous, and I wished that it would never end.

The next morning, I awoke in his arms, sore, sated, and happy. There were many more nights and mornings together as Ferencz would not be called away for another year. In that time, he taught me much about how to manage the servants. All of the servants were afraid of Ferencz. Each of them had received a lashing or two from him in the past. I walked in on him in the middle of the punishment of a servant girl.

"Take off your clothes!" He screamed at the young girl. She didn't move fast enough so he assisted her roughly. He whipped her naked body. First, he bent her over the bedside and whipped her bottom until it bled. I could see he had an erection as he whipped the girl. He stroked himself between lashings.

"No more, my lord, please, no more!" She cried.

"Yes, yes, there will be much more," he assured her in his deep voice. He loosed his fly and let his erection fall free. He thrust himself into her backside and she screamed out in pain into the pillows. He rode the girl hard, and continued to whip her across her back and shoulders.

He looked back and saw me in the doorway. He did not stop molesting the girl, instead he handed me the wooden switch.

"Do whatever you think feels good."

I started to whip the girl, lightly at first. He turned the girl on her side by grabbing a fistful of her hair, his heavy cock still inside of her bottom. I landed a lash across her plump belly, and then across her collar bone. She shrieked. I put the whip down, removed my clothing and got up on the bed with them. I rested the girl's head on my inner thigh. Ferencz smiled as he forced the girl's face into me. She knew all well what to do and did not wish to displease Ferencz anymore. She pleasured me and Ferencz until we were both spent, several times over.

After releasing the girl, Ferencz washed himself and then lay on the bed with me and we slept.

At Orsolya's insistence, I commissioned a painting of myself to be created. I had resisted sitting for a painter, but Orsolya was relentless in her campaign to have my image rendered on canvas.

"We have many beautiful paintings in our residences, both on canvas and in mural form. If I remember correctly, you spent quite a bit of time regarding Ferencz's portrait."

"His was lovely in all aspects. I worry that mine will not come out so well."

"You have nothing to worry about. I will have the family's painter travel from Italy and you will see your inner essence flourish on the canvas."

That is what worries me, I thought.

Several months later, Marco Strozzi Vettici arrived from Venice. I felt uncomfortable around him from the first moment he laid eyes on me. He observed me wherever I went throughout the castle, claiming that he needed to study me in my natural form and manner. I hated being a spectacle, and even when I hid, he always seemed to find me. After two weeks of Marco pursuing me, he finally said he was ready to paint me.

"*Contessa*, please, allow me to capture your true beauty. Have a seat here," he said in his heavy Italian accent. He directed me to a bench across from his easel. I sat for over an hour as he sketched my likeness, humming and murmuring to himself.

"How much longer do you expect you will need me here, Signor Marco?" I was impatient and hated sitting anywhere in one place for so long.

"No worries, *Contessa*, I shall not take up too much of your time."

Four hours later, his brush flew madly across and around the canvas, colors and strokes obeying

Marco's creative will. His brow was knitted and his eyes focused completely on his work. I sat still, my back erect; I did not want to appear as a hunchback in my portrait.

"You may stand now, so that I may capture your lovely gown in this portrait," he directed.

I stood next to a table, and after another hour, he was finally finished. I was exhausted.

"May I look at it?" I asked, feeling like I was owed a quick look after so many hours of tiresome waiting.

"No, no, not yet, *cara mia*. I still have much work to do. I shall let you know when it is ready.

Wearily, I walked upstairs to my chambers, tore off my clothes and collapsed into bed. I did not see Marco again for almost a week, and finally, he emerged from his chambers, looking wearier than I had when I sat for the portrait.

"It is finished. Come, have a look."

He escorted me to his chambers, where upon his easel stood my portrait. I stepped around to the front to view his work, all the while he looked at me expectantly.

I was shocked to see my own eyes staring back at me, clearer than any mirror image I had ever seen. I cannot say that I was thrilled with my image. As vain as I had become, I was not happy with how he painted my face; it was devoid of any affection or emotion. Of course, after several hours of sitting, he probably captured more of my weariness rather than my inner grace. My gown and jewelry looked very realistic; he had painted my hair a bit too dark for my satisfaction. All in all, I was impressed by his skill.

"It is beautiful," was all I could say.

"You approve? I am so happy! I hope that it pleases you, *Contessa*."

"Yes, very much so. It speaks to me in a strange way."

"I hear that often, that the eyes do most of the talking, in a sense."

"You did paint my eyes very well." I turned to him, "Thank you so very much for all of your hard work. You are truly talented."

He took my hands in his own. "You are a lovely subject and it was an honor and a pleasure to be allowed to paint your likeness," he said and then kissed my hand. "I have one other thing for you," he said as he went to retrieve something from a nearby table. He handed me a box, and I opened it to find a miniature portrait, similar to the painting he had just created.

"Thank you, this is very pretty." I fingered the ornate edges of the gilded frame.

"Something for your husband, yes?"

"Yes, he will enjoy having it," I said as I smiled back at him.

A week later, Ferencz was pleased to receive the miniature likeness of me for his birthday.

"This is wonderful. It will allow me to gaze upon your beauty while I am away at war," he said as he looked at my likeness. "Marco is very talented. He captured something of your soul in these paintings."

"You think so? I was very tired after sitting for so long."

"I sat for him when I was younger, but I was so fidgety, he scolded me and sent me from the room!" he laughed.

"I should have fidgeted more, I suppose, because I love your portrait."

"Not more than having me here in person, I hope," he teased.

I walked over to him and threw my arms around his neck, and caressed his broad shoulders. "Never, my love. I want you with me forever."

He leaned down to deliver a kiss, lingering and passionate.

Ferencz left again in the summertime. We had settled the household in at Castle Čachtice in the fall, much to Orsolya's dismay. The castle was surrounded by several villages and farmlands, bordered by the breathtaking views and outcrops of the Carpathian Mountains. Orsolya found many reasons to complain; she did not like Čachtice as it was starkly different from Sárvár—she did not take kindly to change, and like a child, she threw tantrums whenever we moved the household. Čachtice was different in shape, and this bothered Orsolya. Sárvár was a five-sided fortress with a full moat that made her feel safe. She also complained Čachtice was draftier, not well-lit, was built up too high on its precipice, and had no artistic frescoes to ornament its halls as Sárvár had. Nothing pleased her about Čachtice.

Ferencz was away intermittently for the next five years. He received his knighthood and was a highly respected soldier. There was word that he was recommended to be Palatine, just as his father before him.

I exchanged letters with him faithfully over the years that grew from five to ten. I missed his presence dearly and whenever he visited, I kept him all to myself. I looked forward to seeing the messengers as they often brought me Ferencz's letters and news from the field.

My dear wife,

Salutations and good health. We are still at war with the Turks, and engage them in battle often. They are devils. I have killed many, but the bloodshed seems like it will never end. By now, you have heard of my knighthood, of which I am very proud.

I know that you are taking good care of our estates, and business matters. Time stops when I think of you, your beautiful eyes, and your delicious lips. Knowing that I will see you again makes me fight harder to end this war. Be well my love, and dream of me as I dream of you.

Your faithful husband,
Ferencz

Reports of Ferencz's military prowess had spread all over the empire and caught the interest of many nobles and royalty. I was very proud of Ferencz's accomplishments, and I wanted him to be equally proud of me and without worry when it came to matters of our estates.

Dear husband,

I write to you under a sunny sky, which reminds me of times we have walked together in our gardens. I will always hold the picture of you in my mind, smelling the sweet scents of the roses with me.

Know that things are taken care of at

home, and I will be restlessly awaiting your return. Our inventories are well stocked. We've had an abundant harvest and will likely see some superb wines next year. The granaries are full, and we were able to sell our overstock quickly, turning a nice profit.

My love, please tread carefully. I long for you and worry about your health and safety. Come home to me soon.

Your obedient and faithful wife,
Erzsébet

Word had come back from the field that Ferencz had been cheating with many different whores. I smiled to myself when I heard the news. I knew his appetites and after learning from him the great pleasures of sex, it did not bother me. He would always return to me.

Orsolya dined with me often. She did not like being alone in Castle Čachtice.

"My room seems drafty. I care not to be in there by myself."

"Dear mother, I will send the servants up to warm your rooms."

"No, please don't go to the extra trouble. I will make do." It was so like her to be the martyr. "My dear, you've heard from our Ferencz?"

"Yes, he is doing well on the field. He is a knight, now."

"I would expect no less from my son. He is a brilliant strategist. He should be back to visit again soon. Have you and he tried to make children during his visits?"

I blushed at her directness. "No Orsolya, I have

avoided becoming pregnant. After Anastasia, I do not know if I could survive childbirth again."

"You must, my dear. In order to preserve the houses of Nádasdy and Báthory, you must bear children legitimately for succession and inheritance."

"Yes, I know, I will think about it, but know this dear mother, I am no brood mare."

"You should give this much thought. You've been married over ten years and still no children. People have been saying that you are barren."

"Let them talk. We know differently, do we not?" I gave her a knowing look.

Seven

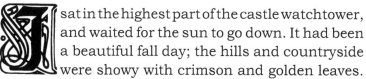I sat in the highest part of the castle watchtower, and waited for the sun to go down. It had been a beautiful fall day; the hills and countryside were showy with crimson and golden leaves. I could hear the howls of the mountain wolves escape the thick vegetation of the nearby forest. A gentle herd of deer grazed in the meadow, unmoved by the hungry calls of their predators.

I felt omnipotent as I observed the grand views of the lofty, steep slopes of the Carpathian Mountains. Carved and cragged rock spurs outcropped from the ground of the surrounding forested valley, and reached straight into the sky. Fingers of light touched their sharp peaks, which would soon be covered in snow.

Some of the castle soldiers were engaged in sword practice, and I could hear the clanking of their swords as steel contacted steel. I fed myself from a decadent platter of well-aged cheese, crusty bread generously spread with olive oil, and sweet, sticky figs alongside a bowl of recently-harvested grapes.

I cleared my mind of the castle business that I had attended to earlier that day. Thoughts of inventories and revenue ledgers would tickle my consciousness if I had allowed the intrusion. My visits to the watchtower were the perfect answer to the peacefulness I sought. For some visits, I would bring a lap harp or a wind whistle, as music calmed my nerves and engaged my mind in artistic thought. Most times, I would bring something to read, such as a stack of Ferencz's letters from the field, or journals sent from the Sárvár presses.

A messenger rode up the steep path to the castle gates on his sturdy brown horse, letter satchel affixed at his side. I ran down to the foyer to receive him. I knew Ferencz would have written and I longed to read his words.

The messenger was a tall and lanky young man with large blue eyes and straight black hair. His features were sharp and overstated, and I longed to bite his full lips as he spoke.

"Greetings, Your Excellency, I am Anton and I bring you correspondence and gifts from His Excellency, your husband," the young messenger said as he bowed deeply and handed me a letter.

"Thank you, please see my notary for your wages and a meal. You are welcome to stay within the castle this evening. I will have a response to send to my husband in the morning."

"Yes, Your Excellency, I would be honored to rest here this night. I will unsaddle the gifts from His Excellency and have them brought in to you."

Practically running, I headed for my chambers, locked the doors and tore open Ferencz's letter.

Greetings to my beloved wife,

I write this letter from my encampment, stationed somewhere in the middle of nowhere. It has been several days since we have encountered the enemy, so my troops are at rest. I thought I would put this idle time to good use and write to you.

I wonder what activities your days are filled with. Do you think of me as I think of you? I can only imagine what it is like to run our estates. I was never trained in the art of running a castle by Mother. I am most happy that you are adept at managing everything, while I fight to preserve it.

My days are filled with war. If it is not direct battle, then it is strategy and planning. We move around a great deal. It is a challenge to manage hundreds of young troops, traveling to so many different venues, while keeping the spirit and morale up as is needed. These boys were born to fight. They attack and engage in battle with much vigor.

When I return, what do you think about trying to have children? I know that you have had a bad experience in the past, but think about the advantages that having children would bring to us. I am sure that Mother has been pressuring you, but aside from that, it would please me greatly if you would be the mother of my children.

From the time of our betrothal when we were both just youths, I knew that I needed someone like you at my side. Erzsébet, my beautiful darling wife, you have made me the most happiest of men, just simply by being my wife. Children would make our eternal bond complete. Please think about it and consider my request.

Along with this letter, I am sending to you some gifts I have found for you in my travels. The first is a book of poetry, written in the French tongue. I have read it many times, and I wish for you to enjoy it as much as I have. Next, I am sending some lovely tapestries and hangings we have collected from some of the defeated Turkish encampments. I hope that you enjoy them. Lastly, I am sending you a small cache of Turkish jewelry, worn by some of the commanders of their army. Please have our jeweler make something that will adorn your beautiful person before my return.

I am looking forward to returning home soon, to your warm embrace and loving eyes. Be well, my beauty and look to the horizon for my homecoming.

Your faithful husband,
Ferencz

I wrote Ferencz a letter that evening. It took me several hours and many drafts to conjure a proper response after rereading his letter many times.

Should I tell him that I wish to remain childless? Should I be a dutiful and obedient wife and give him the heirs he so longs for? The prospect of having children with Ferencz seemed like the right thing to do. After all, that is why we were married. Our love for each other was just an added treasure.

I wondered how much Orsolya's influence had played into Ferencz's forwardness about the subject. For many years, he was just as contented as I not to have children running about underfoot, or at least that is what I assumed. *No,* I thought, *I must do the right thing and give Ferencz what he wants.* I wrote the letter, sealing my decision and my fate.

To my cherished husband,

Greetings and good health to you. I am very pleased with the gifts you have sent from the field. It was most generous for you to think of me. I will have the jeweler make us both some attractive rings from the gems you sent. I hope that you will be very satisfied with their settings. Orsolya and I both enjoyed the tapestries, and I am reading the poetry book. What a clever poet!

I think of you everyday, my darling husband. I relish in the thoughts of our times together, our days and our nights. I look for your return everyday, and I take great pride in knowing that we both work with one another to further the prosperity of our lives. You fight to protect your country while I manage the fruits of your labors. Orsolya is an excellent teacher and I continue to learn from her each day. You are the sum of your parents' best traits, of that I am certain.

I have thought long about your proposal to have children. I have lingered too long with the notion of being childless for the rest of my life. I do want to have your children—otherwise, what is the purpose of all our hard work and efforts? I would be honored to have your children, and I will go through whatever pains I must endure to see to it that our family line is carried on.

Of course, in order to have children, you must be here, dear husband! I look forward to your arrival, and even though childbirth is a great burden, making children with you will be my life's greatest pleasure.

I took to my bed last month with an illness the apothecary called influenza. I felt terrible, but am better now. I pray that you never have this ailment. I was achy all over my body, my throat hurt, and I had a persistent fever. Zoran prescribed some inhalants and herbs which worked wonders, but warned me that this ailment is very contagious. I do hope that it will have passed out of the castle before your arrival.

Darvulia and my servants have kept me company, along with your mother. I worry about your mother as she spends a large amount of time by herself. I shall keep you *updated if she falls ill. We turned a nice profit on wine this year; our vineyards were some of the heartiest last season. Ficko recently informed me that your favorite mare has given birth to a fine young colt.*

I will await your return from my perch in the watchtower. I go there almost everyday as it is one of the few places I may be alone with my thoughts. Rest assured that I will not let you down in my position as mistress of our estates. You will find everything in perfect order upon your return.

Please, return to me soon, my love.

Your obedient and faithful wife,
Erzsébet

Ferencz's response to my letter came right away, by way of the same messenger, Anton.

To Erzsébet, my treasured wife,

Soon after I last wrote to you, our rest was interrupted by a skirmish with the Turks. They are relentless demons; greedy for land and whatever else they can place their vile hands upon. We chased the cowards through several small villages along the border of Hungary and Bulgaria, all the while they were raping and torturing women and children, burning down buildings, and plundering valuable harvests. I loathe the Turks! I will make sure that they all know my wrath.

Enough about war. I am glad that you are recovered from your influenza. It is an ailment that should not be taken lightly. There have been outbreaks that have wiped out entire cities, and it is almost as bad as the plague. Please do take care of yourself, and do not worry about me. If I hear that the sickness has not left the castle by the time of my arrival, I will send word to you of my whereabouts and remain away until it is safe to return.

I am delighted about your decision to have our children. Knowing this makes me want to push harder to get home to you, my love. I received word from Mother. I do believe you are right that she is not herself, but she did not tell me of any maladies. I hope that you do keep a watchful eye over her, and make sure she gets any care necessary to sustain her health. I do not wish to lose her; it would be different than it was when Father died. I hardly knew him, but I cherish Mother.

Have you had any word from your parents? It was nice of them to visit us last winter, and I hope that we might travel to see them soon.

I venture to guess that I will be returning

home within the next month. In fact, you may receive this letter after I make it back! I shall pay the horseman extra to deliver this letter with great haste.

Be well, darling. My heart is yours, always.

Your husband,
Ferencz

After reading Ferencz's last letter, my heart beat faster in anticipation of his arrival. *We were to make children!* Up until then, our couplings were for mutual pleasure. I was nervous at the prospect of bearing another child. I remembered the vivid details of Anastasia's birth—the lack of dignity and pain of that birth would never leave my mind.

Eight

arsh icy winds froze Hungary the winter my father died. The deep freeze lasted for many months, and I thought it would never end. I began my visit with Father and Mother at Castle Ecsed in the fall and extended my visit when I discovered that they had both been ill. I was angered that no one had sent word to me. Mother was not her illustrious self, and was dressed in a gray wool loose gown, her hair was unkempt and discolored with streaks of gray. Her face was bloated and her lips were covered with oozing sores. I felt sorry for her that she had lost her beauty and I thought about my own looks. I decided the moment I saw her that I did not want to ever look like her. I studied my face for hours in her looking glass, searching for features we held in common. She sat next to Father, whispering to herself some unknowable secret. She would giggle and then look around as if she were lost. She did not recognize me when I arrived, and throughout my visit, she had forgotten my name and referred to me as if I were a servant.

Even though Father had shown the signs of age, he had done so more gracefully, and he did not look as haggard as Mother. He sat in his favorite throne for so many months that his legs atrophied. He rocked himself and mumbled poetry over and over again; sometimes tears would fill his eyes.

I looked at my parents, seated side by side, and felt enormous grief that either of them had to live at all in their conditions. My father was once one of the most powerful men in all of Hungary and he was reduced to a drooling, infantile idiot, whose servants had to feed him his meals and change him when he soiled himself.

One morning, just after the first snow, I awoke and found him slumped over in his throne, eyes open and not breathing. I felt relief that he had passed. He was interred next to my sisters in our family crypt. I visited the three of them before I left Ecsed. My sisters' bodies had degenerated to bones, but their hair still held the same beautiful colors of their youth. I picked up Sondra's skeletal hand and the attached arm fell free as it was raised. Her skull seemed to smile at me as I studied the hollowed eye sockets. I wondered what had happened to all of her flesh. The ravages of time are never merciful on the dead—or the living.

I touched my face and felt the soft supple skin beneath my fingers. My mind began to race with thoughts of death and decay on my own person and I pictured myself on the crypt slab next to my father. His flesh had already begun to stink, and his skin was as cold as the slab beneath him.

Erzsébet, I thought I had heard him whisper my name. I could not understand what was real and what my imagination had conjured. In that pocket of time, it seemed fathomable that my sisters would arise to dance among our ancestor's bones and welcome Father to the tomb. My mind produced a horrifying image of him reaching over to me and I ran screaming out of the crypt.

I had calmed myself after several hours and I went to visit Mother one last time. When I left, I knew I would not see Mother alive again. In a sense, she was already gone, and the servants assured me they would lay her to rest next to Father and send word to me. The following spring, I received word that she had finally passed.

Ferencz returned home for a brief stay in the springtime of 1584. As always, our reuniting was passionate, as if we both had to satisfy a deep and urgent thirst. I would often use herbal remedies to ensure that I would not become pregnant during my sexual adventures, with Ferencz or anyone else. This time, I decided to forgo their use and I allowed myself to become pregnant. I suddenly felt a strong desire to become a mother, especially after considering his plea to start a family. I wondered about Anastasia often, and the thought had crossed my mind to find her.

That summer, just after my morning sicknesses had resolved, I made the long journey back to Ecsed to find Danijel and Anastasia. I cloaked myself in a simple gown of brown wool—something the wife of a merchant would wear, well below my station—and took Darvulia and Ficko with me for the venture.

When we arrived in Ecsed, I visited my family crypt and said my words of closing to my mother. She was dressed in a garnet gown, with makeup applied to her face and her hair dressed and ornamented with golden ribbons. Death had been kinder to her looks than life had been in the end. I looked over at Father, and the bones of my sisters. The flesh of Father's face had decayed and sunk to cling to his bones like a tough leathery mask. Their hands were joined in the same manner that Father had always taken her hand in life. I had the tomb door sealed behind me by the grounds keeper. I hoped I would never see the crypt again, in life or death.

Darvulia and Ficko waited patiently for me in the carriage. When Darvulia began to speak, I raised my hand to silence her and no one said a word as we left the crypt. We found a room at an inn on the outskirts of the village. The streets swarmed with people trading and buying goods at the market. Both sides of the streets were lined with merchant booths of every type. There was an abundance of fresh fruit and vegetables, hearty baked breads and delicate pastries, dried and salted meats, mead and ale. We sampled something from almost every merchant, and we packed a large quantity of food for the trip back to Čachtice. The wonderful smells and tastes from the market had awakened some incessant cravings for various foods, and I became quite colicky and temperamental without them.

Throughout our walk, I searched for a wine vendor. I had hoped Danijel or his father still lived in Ecsed. If they did, the market would be one of the places where they would sell their goods. At the end of the day, I felt deflated; we had seen many wine merchants but we had not found Danijel or Anastasia.

"Why don't we take a rest and have some tea and a massage for you, my lady? You look tired and I think you should rest," Darvulia offered.

"Yes, I think you are right. I would like my feet massaged." My ankles and feet were swollen up much larger than normal by the end of the day.

We were directed to a local midwife named Brigit,

and were warmly welcomed when we arrived at her home. She examined me and had her daughter elevate my feet and massage my shoulders. Brigit was a heavy-set lady with long brown hair, dressed well in a burgundy wool gown. She had large brown eyes, a charming full-lipped smile and a warm touch. I felt comfortable allowing her to examine and care for me.

"Anastasia, would you please get our patron a cup of sweet tea?" Brigit directed her daughter to fetch my drink. The young girl was lovely. She had a winsome and dreamy look about her, with large brown eyes and a healthy head of wavy auburn hair. Her skin was perfect, and her voice was soft and melodic.

"How old is your beautiful daughter?"

"She just turned ten. She's actually not my daughter by birth, but my step-daughter. Her father and I were married only last year."

I sat back and enjoyed my tea and surveyed the young girl as she worked on my swollen feet and achy shoulders.

"What does your father do, my dear?" I asked the girl.

"He is a wine merchant, my lady. Right now he is at the seaport taking care of a shipment to France." My heart felt like it had stopped beating. Her father had to be Danijel. She had to be my child—my Anastasia. Her eyes were down cast in pious humility. She did not have a rebellious streak as I had.

"He has been such a Godsend to me, that man. I love him so very much for giving me the family I've always wanted," Brigit said.

"How so?"

"I am barren, and also widowed. Danijel was a cousin of my husband." I was shocked when I heard Brigit speak his name. She continued, "When Ján died, I was alone and Danijel comforted me. He and Anastasia needed me and I needed them."

She seemed so happy. Blissful and unaware. I could not bring myself to tear apart their happy world, no matter how much I longed to hold my Anastasia. I looked at Anastasia one last time before leaving. I bit my tongue so hard that I tasted blood.

"May your family have much happiness and prosperity. Thank you so much for your hospitality." I motioned to Darvulia to pay Brigit. We left her enough gold florins for a year's worth of work, and I could hear her squeal in delight when we left.

A moment later she was at her door while we boarded our carriage. "My lady, please come back, you've paid me overmuch, and I cannot accept this."

"This visit was worth every bit, for reasons which you will never know. Please send my salutations to Danijel."

"May I ask your name, my lady?"

"Erzsébet. Just Erzsébet."

After a large and clumsy pregnancy, and two days' worth of labor, Anna was finally born in December, and I called her my Christmas present from Ferencz. She was a beautiful baby with a light crest of red hair and fair skin. I nursed her myself, even though I had a wet nurse available at my whim.

I was very protective of Anna. I did not want anyone to take her as Anastasia had been taken. I would not allow anyone to hold her, not even Orsolya, and I was stricken with fear that she would not thrive and be healthy, or that she would be stolen away as I slept.

I kept to myself in my chambers, drapes drawn shut, Anna at my side in her bed. For many months,

I allowed only Darvulia and Katalin in to my rooms, and I would not speak. I fell into a deep depression, and thought often of my own demise.

Ferencz visited the following spring. He expertly cantered through the castle gates, handsomely mounted on his muscular white horse. He wore his onyx-black armor with the Báthory-Nádasdy coat of arms inlaid in gold. The church bells sounded upon his arrival and I remembered my reason for living. He lifted my spirits and showed his great love for our child. Depression had relaxed its tight grip on my psyche and I felt more relaxed about motherhood.

Anna grew fast, and toddled around the castle, her governess in close proximity at all times. Ferencz chased her, tickled and tossed her as she squealed gleefully. I adored him even more as I watched him with our daughter. Ferencz was known as a fearsome fighter, a tyrannical master to his servants, but with Anna, he was protective, tender and loving. I watched him as he cuddled and kissed her as she sat on his lap, her fat little fingers intertwined in his hair.

It saddened me greatly when he had to leave on another tour of duty. Ferencz worried for my safety as the Turks had turned their attention to Sárvár while he was away, although our forces there had kept them at bay and they did little damage to the local villages. The battles seemed unreal to me until I had heard of this skirmish.

"I would feel much safer if you, Anna and Mother remained here at Čachtice until I return. The Turks have been testing our resources in the Sárvár region and I do not wish you to become trapped there."

"We will remain here until your return, dear husband." I touched his cheek and looked deep into his eyes. Those dark pools of lust and passion, of ferocity and cruelty. I wondered how many deaths had those eyes seen. Yet when he looked at me, his eyes were full of love and longing. Ferencz was enigmatic.

After Ferencz left for his duty, I checked in on Orsolya frequently. She spent most of her time within her chambers, and would not eat any of her meals. She had a sickly pallor to her skin, and drifted into sleep often. I watched her doze, and wondered how long it would be before she died. She was propped up in her bed and her head was tilted back a bit. She snored lightly between labored breaths, and there was a line of foul-smelling drool that dripped from her mouth.

I brought in my apothecary Zoran to examine her, much to her dislike. She thought the man was evil as he was well-practiced in the arts of the occult. After much argument, she finally consented to allow his examination. She complained of pain in her mouth, which is why she would not eat her meals.

"Please open your mouth, madam. I must see inside to find out what ails you." He turned her chin up gently as he inspected her teeth and gums. Her breath was awful and he turned away briefly to catch a deep breath of clean air.

"Mind your manners!" she snapped at him.

"My apologies, Your Excellency. It would seem that you have a cyst beneath one of your teeth, toward the upper area in the back of your mouth. This is what has caused the odor and your pain."

"A cyst? Can you repair this?" she asked.

"I will apply a salve to the cyst and you will need to have it reapplied each day. The swelling should go down in a few days. I will also call for the leechman to bleed you."

Orsolya scoffed at the mention of leeches. "I have no need for the loss of any blood! No leechman!"

"As you wish, madam," Zoran knew not to argue with Orsolya. He took me aside in the hallway.

"How is she, really?"

"If the cyst ruptures, or if there is malignity within it, she could die. Feed her only soft mashed foods and see that she has plenty of rest. I will return in a week's time."

"Thank you, Zoran."

"It is always my pleasure to serve this great noble family. Send for me if there are any changes."

Orsolya developed a high fever and sweats soon after Zoran had left. She was fitful and would not eat. Her priest arrived and spent many hours lingering over her, reading her scriptures. Delirious and hallucinogenic, her mind played many tricks on her.

"Tamas, please come home. No more war, just be with me," she called to her late husband. I took her hand and she looked at me and then realized that I was not Tamas. She slapped me hard across the cheek and I got up and left her bedside.

Orsolya died that afternoon. Her sheets were soaked with sweat and urine. I had her bed destroyed and Orsolya was placed in the castle morgue.

"Darvulia, please send word to Ferencz that his mother has passed."

"Yes, my lady."

Ferencz wrote a week later:

> *My dearest wife who holds my heart,*
>
> *I am sorry that I could not make it back before Mother passed away. My heart is*

heavy with sadness that I will never behold her again. She was a brilliant woman, whom I revered. Please take care of her body and move it to Sárvár. I shall travel there within a months' time and survey her remains.

Your loving husband,
Ferencz

I hired a mortician to prepare Orsolya's body for the journey to Sárvár. He cleansed her body, and embalmed it using spices, wax and unguents. Ficko assisted me in transporting Orsolya's body. Ferencz sent several soldiers who were stationed nearby Čachtice, to accompany us to Sárvár.

Upon our arrival at Sárvár, I spent many hours deliberating on what clothing I should select for Orsolya's interment. I decided on a simple black wool gown and a strand of pearls. I had argued with the notion of sending her off in one of my more illustrious gowns, but decided against it. Simple was more her style than mine.

Ficko collected her body from the morgue, and placed her in the Nádasdy crypt after a short funeral. After the crowd of mourners dispersed, I found myself again in a crypt.

Orsolya was laid next to Tamas, Ferencz's father. Tamas passed away when Ferencz was just a small child. Ferencz had three siblings, who had all died young. I observed them in death. Their little bodies were wrapped tightly, mummified by time, and they were laid to rest near their other relatives. My heart felt sadness for Orsolya's loss of her children, and I realized why she had prized Ferencz and his accomplishments with such enthusiasm.

When I returned to Čachtice, I retired to my chambers and ordered the servants to stay away, even Darvulia. I wished to be alone. I was consumed with thoughts of death, turning the notion over in my mind, imagining gruesome thoughts.

I dreamt that I had died, but I was still alive and trapped within my rotting body. I could not move or speak, yet all my senses were keen. I was placed in the cold castle morgue. Ficko washed my naked body. He cleansed and massaged my skin with natural oils. I was dead to him, yet I saw his erection as he cleaned me. He wrapped me in a crisp white shroud and left the room. I began to feel my skin rot all around me, the stink rising to my nose. My soul could not claw its way out of the rotting corpse, and I was left there, screaming within. I could taste the metallic flavor of blood within my mouth, but I could not swallow. I could feel coldness throughout my body, but I could not shiver. I could see the empty room around me, but I could not shut my eyes. Ficko returned to the room, this time with suturing tools. He had Darvulia with him and they stitched my mouth and eyes shut, which was customary before a funeral. I could feel the searing pain of the needle and thread being drawn through the thin skin of my eye lids and lips, but I could not scream out in protest.

My body was moved to rest on top of a stone slab in a silent room filled with musty, unmoving air. The coldness of the slab crept up and stole any remaining warmth left within my body. I heard a heavy door shut and then there was total silence. Pestilence was the only living thing inside the room, and I could feel it crawl over and within me. My skin tingled and itched. It was as if the creatures were waiting for my arrival and they greedily consumed my body until there was nothing left but bones. My soul was released and I felt myself floating, light as a feather, within the crypt above my body, and over the bodies of Orsolya's family. They all sat up and reached for me, but I floated out of their grasp, floated away.

I awoke with a scream, and I sat upright, drenched in sweat.

Nine

ate decided I had not had my fair share of death, for my uncle Stefan, King of Poland and Prince of Transylvania died late in the year of 1586. I had fond memories of Stefan, as he was always a kind soul to me throughout my childhood. He often brought me toys and games from faraway places, and would spend hours playing and laughing with me.

I attended Stefan's funeral in Krakow, Poland. His wife, Queen Anna Jagiellon sat in her pew solemnly, under a dark veil. Stefan was interred in the Mariacka Chapel, within the Cathedral of Saint Mary. It was a wondrous cathedral that housed the grand Altar of Saint Stanislaus. Stained glass depicted Polish saints. Tall pillar candles and dark wood panels and railings surrounded the great altar. There was a comforting scent of frankincense and myrrh in the air, which mingled with chants of monks.

Ferencz met me at the funeral and sat alongside of me during the service. I could hardly pay attention to the priest as he read Stefan's eulogy, for I was enthralled with Ferencz, whom I hadn't seen in over a year. He had grown a rougher look; his hair was longer, his skin coarser and darker, but he was still the man I loved.

Much to my delight, Ferencz joined me in the carriage

on the way back to Castle Čachtice. Finally, alone with him, I drank him in.

"I am most happy to be back with you, dear wife. How is our daughter?"

"She is healthy, happy. Her governess is taking excellent care of her. Will you stay at Čachtice very long?" I hated the thought of his departure so soon after his arrival.

"Yes, I should be able to stay for a while. We have whipped the Turks into submission, so I believe our surrounding fortresses are safe, for now. They took a great loss in this last skirmish. I was also granted the title of Chief Commander over the entire Hungarian garrison."

"I am so proud of you, my husband, and I feel safer knowing that you have fought them off, but I also feel much safer knowing you are with me, protecting me." He took my hand in his and smiled. I blushed. Even after so many years of marriage, he had the power to make me redden with a simple look.

"How did the funeral for Mother turn out? Were there many people in attendance?"

"It was a small ceremony, just as I believe she would have liked. Her closest friends paid their condolences. I am sorry that you were away when such a dreadful thing happened."

"Yes, I feel guilty that I was not at her side when she died. Tell me, was she in much pain?"

"No, I don't believe so. Zoran aided her with herbs and teas. She seemed at peace after his remedies were applied."

Ferencz withdrew for a few moments, likely deep in thought over his mother. I watched the scenery pass by as our carriage moved swiftly down the path. The land was ready for its winter sleep, tired of bearing fruit to its people for the year. I felt tired, tired of so much death.

Ferencz, seated across from me, moved over to my side of the carriage. He drew the drapes shut and smothered me with warm kisses. We managed to make love in the moving carriage without either of us undressing. Heated and primal were his movements and I felt like a ray of light had touched my soul when we were both spent from our exertions of lovemaking.

I enjoyed all of the attention I received from Ferencz when I discovered I was pregnant with our second child. He was home for the winter, and possibly for the following year.

"Everyone shall obey you. You are mistress of this house. I shall not tolerate any disobedience," Ferencz said to me, in front of a line of servants, reminding them of his power. "Anyone who does not obey shall be severely punished by me."

I witnessed his fury released on two chambermaids that afternoon. He caught them giggling about my burden of weight from my pregnancy. When I heard their screams, I ran into the hallway, where Ferencz had them on their knees.

"Damn you! Damn you both to hell! You shall not speak of my wife, your mistress in that way!" Ferencz slapped both girls repeatedly until their noses and mouths bled.

His manservant, Derosh stood by, waiting for direction. "Move these girls to my quarters," he commanded. "Dear wife," he spotted me watching, "please come with me to observe their punishment."

I followed the girls, Ferencz and Derosh into Ferencz's suite, and sat on a Turkish divan. The girls cried out loudly, and Ferencz responded with more ferocity, slapping them down to the ground. Derosh ripped off their clothing, and left them naked before their master.

Ferencz retrieved a whip from his dressing table. It was no ordinary whip, but one that had small pieces of metal affixed to the leather. With a loud crack, the whip came down on the legs of the girls, drawing a rough line of blood from their creamy skin.

"Would you like a turn, my lovely?" He handed me the whip and I obliged him. I cracked the whip down on the back of one girl, and then across the front of the other. The rush of the power I held over the two stupid little brats excited me.

"Derosh, tie these girls up for their next round of punishment."

Derosh tied one girl to a chair, with her legs spread wide, and the other girl to Ferencz's bed. They both had lovely breasts, now marred with blood from the brutal lashings. Ferencz motioned to me over to the bed. I went over to one side of the bed and bent down to study the breasts of the lithe little blonde. She looked up at me, terrified of what I would do. I bit into the velvety smooth flesh of one breast, and gnawed fiercely at her pale pink nipple for a while. She cried out and tried to get away, but Ferencz slapped her face. Ferencz unfastened his breeches and proceeded to mount the girl. As he rode her she cried out in protest.

"Please master, I am sorry, I will obey your orders, please don't—"

"You little bitch! You stupid insolent swine!" He slapped her across the face and continued to roughly take what he wanted.

I took a lit candle and I singed the pubic hair of the hefty brunette who was tied to the chair. She screamed out as the flame scorched her skin and delicate pink pubis. The smell of her burned hair and skin filled the air and mingled with the scent of the hot wax that I allowed to drip across her body and onto her face.

When we had finished torturing the girls, Derosh untied them and led them down to a subterranean vault within the castle, where Ferencz ordered them to be boiled in front of the rest of the servants.

"Make sure all of them attend, I want to be sure they all understand the consequences of disobedience to their masters," he said as he cleaned himself off and pulled up his breeches.

We ventured down to the vault and watched as Ficko assisted Derosh in binding the girls. A cauldron of water sat atop of lit kindling and logs. Small waves of rolling bubbles were produced on the surface of the water. The girls were then lowered into the boiling water in front of the line of servants. Darvulia smiled as the girls screamed, while other servants turned their heads away. The corpses were left in the forest for the wolves, and were devoured completely in less than a day.

There were very few incidents of disobedience while Ferencz was within the castle. My pregnancy was going smoothly, and I felt a great deal of activity within my womb. The August heat had made me quite uncomfortable, and my maids were kept busy keeping me cool.

For my birthday that year, Ferencz had a grand feast made in my honor to celebrate the impending birth of our child. The cooks had outdone themselves, likely in fear of Ferencz. There were decadent meat pies and pastries, rich dishes of paprikash and venison stew, fish quenelles, fresh fruits and honey, figs and dates, and an endless supply of sweet mead.

I was contentedly full and was happy to retire to

sleep after the grand feast.

The day after the feast, I was rendered helpless by my falling sickness. Darvulia gave me herbs to help me sleep, and I did not awaken for three days.

When I awoke, the room seemed to spin around me, and I could not stand on my own. For several days, my throat was dry and raw, and I could not speak. I noticed that there had been no more stirring within my womb. Something felt terribly wrong. I called for Zoran to be brought to me.

"Your belly is quite large for your term, my lady," Zoran felt around my stomach and examined me from all angles.

"I have been with child six months."

"Yes, that would be about right, but I think you may have twin souls within your womb."

I was shocked. "Two babies? But why is there no movement? I am sure there was much movement before my last episode."

"Yes, there should be a great deal of movement as the children fight for room for themselves in such a small space. It is my recommendation that you stay in your bed for a few weeks. I want to make sure you do not over exert yourself." He handed Darvulia some herbs and assured me he would return in a week.

Several days had passed, and I was in great pain. Cramps gripped my belly and I started to bleed. I experienced another fit of my sickness, and when I awoke, Darvulia delivered terrible news.

"My mistress, you have lost the children to the gods. They are within you no more."

My babies were gone. More death than I cared to think about. They were expelled from my womb, wanted by the gods for some purpose we would never know or understand. Darvulia had confirmed Zoran's guess that there were two little fetuses.

"Did you keep them?"

"Yes, I thought you might like to see them."

She led me to the infirmary. My two children, a boy and a girl, lay next to each other, and were swaddled in soft blankets. They had been cleaned and looked as if they were asleep. There was no sweet breath, no tender cooing from their tiny bodies. They were motionless, as if time had stopped; just long enough for me to see them before their departure from this world.

I picked them up, one at a time and held them for several moments, rocking and kissing each of them. "Orsolya and András. May you rest in peace. I am glad you will never know the pain and suffering of this world." I turned and left the infirmary, and joined Ferencz in the gardens.

"My sweet wife, I am so sorry for this pain," he held me tightly, "there will be more children, and they will be healthy and have much vigor," he promised.

"More deaths. It feels like it is beyond my ability to accept. I am glad I was asleep, I would not have wanted to be awake when they were born dead."

"I was there. Darvulia called to me when she saw that you were bleeding profusely. I stayed by your side the entire time. I prayed that they would live, prayed for them to breathe, but the divine powers denied my request."

"You are right," I smiled up at him weakly, "there will be other children. I want to try again as soon as I am recovered."

"Yes, of course we will my sweet. In fact, you should be in bed resting right now." He took my hand and gently led me back to my chambers. With Ferencz's assistance, I got back into bed and stayed there for several weeks. He brought me fresh flowers each day and ordered the servants to bring me anything I desired.

While in my bed, I thought much about my life. I was grateful for my station, being Ferencz's wife. I wielded much power throughout Hungary. I was known as a shrewd businesswoman and an excellent governess of my estates. I had much respect from the nobility of Hungary. I thought about my mother and father, my childhood and the things in my life that made me who I was. My thoughts raced. *Was I a result of my environment? Was I the result of my own thoughts? Or was I just a result of a traumatic youth? Why did I enjoy the torture of others? Why did I revel in their pain?* Questions for which I had no answers. I was always greedy for knowledge, eager to experience everything, but yet I had no idea what propelled my licentious tastes.

Ferencz spent many nights with me once I was recovered. It didn't take long before I realized I was pregnant again. Emperor Rudolf had sent for Ferencz to plan a new campaign against the Turks. Ferencz left for his tour of duty, and wrote me many letters showing his concern for my health.

He would not be disappointed, as I gave birth to our daughter, Katalin, that summer. I knew Ferencz wanted a son, but he was grateful for a healthy birth. He would get his wish as the birth of our son followed a few years later. Ferencz named him Paul, and there was much merriment over our boy's birth. In Paul, Ferencz held the hope of the future of the Nádasdy line. Ferencz coddled the boy and bounced him on his knee.

"I shall teach you to be a brave and fearless fighter," he whispered to Paul. I smiled as I watched the two of them. Paul would gaze into Ferencz's eyes and smile a toothless grin when Ferencz spoke to him.

While Ferencz was back from his recent tour of duty, he had brought his close friend, Miklós Palffy, to stay with us at Čachtice for several months. Miklós was a well-known fighter, much like Ferencz, and they had battled against the Turks for many years together. They were brothers in arms, and had much in common.

Ferencz shared servant girls with Miklós, but never offered to include me in their trysts. This irritated me, as Ferencz had always invited me when he needed to satisfy his carnal urges.

I felt a streak of jealousy, not for the servant girls, but for Miklós. He took up much of Ferencz's time while he was home, which I resented. Ferencz couldn't say enough good things about the man, but I viewed him as a nuisance. I looked forward to his departure, even though it meant Ferencz would be gone as they would leave together for their next skirmish with the Turks.

Miklós approached me in the gardens one day. The sun shined brightly, enhancing the brilliant reddish tone of my hair, and Miklós reached out to touch it.

"What are you doing, sir?"

"Admiring the beauty as it is touched by the fingers of the gods."

"I will thank you not to touch my person ever again."

"As you wish, my lady. Thank you for your kindness in allowing me to stay here at Čachtice with your husband."

"It is not of my doing. Ferencz is the one you should be thanking."

"No, my lady, I thank you for allowing time spent

with my best friend. He is truly a brilliant soul," he said with humbleness. I tried to ignore him, but he was persistently trying to melt the ice around me. He stroked his red beard and looked at me with small brown eyes. He was a little man, stout in stance.

"I must be getting back up to the castle, good day to you, sir."

"No, wait." I tried to leave but he grabbed my wrist, "Please do not go, I would like a few more words with you."

"What pray tell would you like to say?" I did not unleash his grasp of my wrist.

"You are a beautiful woman, my lady."

"Yes, I know. And I am also the wife of your best friend, may I remind you."

"Ah, yes, there is that. Just know that I find you to be just as every bit brilliant as Ferencz." He released his grip on my wrist and I backed away.

"Thank you, now I shall take my leave of you." I did not give him the chance to counter, and I left as fast as I could. The man gave me chills.

Later, while I was in my chambers, Ferencz came in to see me.

"I want to thank you, Erzsébet. You are my prize, my most faithful and valuable possession," he kissed my hand and then my cheek.

"To what do I owe these compliments?"

"You have proven yourself to be a loyal wife. Miklós explained to me that he had feelings for you and that he had approached you in the garden," he said.

So, I thought, *it was a test of my faithfulness.* "I would never bring shame to you, my husband."

"I would not expect you to be so faithful, especially seeing that I am gone so much of the time."

"I understand. If I am ever to choose another man

for pleasure, it would be discreet."

"I hope that I please you, even after all of these years together."

"Nothing makes me happier than to see you come home. My allegiance shall always be to you."

"And I to you, dear wife. No matter what whore, or dalliance, you hold my heart, forever." His dark eyes penetrated into my soul. "Would you like Miklós as a lover while he is here?"

"No, he does not interest me. However, I would like to know why you have not included me in your trysts with the servants? I felt a bit left out," I said petulantly.

He laughed, "Of course you may be with us. Honestly, I did not want to share you with him," he said with a broad smile.

"Thank you, and fear not, he is incapable of winning me over. I find him to be a bore," I assured Ferencz.

That evening, Ferencz invited me into his chambers. Miklós was there, and they had a servant girl brought in. I recognized her as one of the girls who worked in the kitchen. Her name was Ilona, and she was a buxom girl with dark brown hair. Miklós was already working on undressing the girl when I arrived. She seemed worried when I appeared, but then realized that I would be a participant in the meeting.

Her large breasts were loosed from her corset, and her simple skirt fell to the floor. She had a plump body, not unlike a cherub, and was not embarrassed to show it. She placidly mounted Miklós who stretched across the bed. Ferencz entered her other orifice from behind and he motioned me over to the bed. I disrobed and lay next to Miklós, just far enough up on the pillows to allow Ilona to pleasure me. Ferencz caressed my breasts and kissed me passionately while Ilona licked me into a heated frenzy. When I was spent, I leaned back on the bed and watched the men take their pleasure. The girl knelt in front of the men, and sucked them to the heights of ecstasy. Ferencz took her by the hair roughly as he forced himself down her throat. She choked a bit, but obediently took him, and then Miklós. As I watched, I was reminded of my episode with the dark man during Strinennia, years before.

"Did I please you, master? Do you want me to come back later tonight?" Ilona asked. I felt the heat rise in my face. *How dare she? She was not his sole pleasure toy. She was there by my allowance!*

"No, do not come back. We do not require your services anymore this evening," Miklós told the girl as he pulled his breeches up.

I called for Darvulia and we escorted the girl from Ferencz's chambers. He smiled at me as we left. I think he knew what I was going to do to her for her insolence.

"You are such a sweet girl, so sweet to offer your services to my dear husband," I said in a syrupy tone. The girl looked scared. Ficko was waiting for us in my chambers.

"Bind this girl, and see that she does not escape," I told Ficko. Darvulia assisted him in lacing rope around her hands and feet, and then she produced a pot of honey. I brushed the sticky substance all over her body.

"What are you doing to me, my mistress? I hope that I have not displeased you," she said, with worry.

"Silence," I said peacefully, and I continued with my task. "Take her out to the giant oak and tie her to it," I whispered to Ficko when I had finished.

He nodded and then unbound the girl's feet and led her outside, where he and Darvulia tied her to the base of the tree.

Ilona's face turned fearful, "Please, let me go, I don't understand how I've displeased you, Mistress," the girl pleaded. I turned and left with Darvulia and Ficko. Ilona screamed into the dark night as bugs and spiders were attracted to her honey-painted naked body.

The next day, Ilona whimpered as she saw me approach the tree with Darvulia. Stinging ants covered her and she had welts on many areas of her body. I allowed her release and she never approached Ferencz again.

Ten

he following spring, Ferencz and Miklós prepared to leave for their next tour of duty. Ferencz seemed charged with energy, ready to fight against the enemies.

"We shall conquer the devils of the Ottoman Empire! They will regret stepping foot on our sweet soil!" Ferencz was zealous as he packed his weapons and donned his armor.

"I doubt this will be their last time visiting, but we will always be here, ready to fight." Miklós was more subdued than Ferencz, but still anxious to go to battle.

Ferencz turned to me and simply stared into my eyes. I could not look away from his handsomeness, and he saw my tears.

"Do not cry, my beloved, I shall return."

"I know, my love, but I worry every time you leave."

"When I return, we shall visit Vienna together. I want to show you many things in that beautiful city." He kissed my forehead and held me close.

"I would enjoy a trip like that with you. I will watch for your return."

He turned and mounted his horse, and rode out of the castle gates, Miklós at his side. I admired Ferencz as his powerful white horse took him down the path away from the castle. There was an intense energy about Ferencz that, coupled with his chiseled features and muscular physique, brought forth more beauty each time I regarded him.

I moved the household back to Sárvár before winter froze the world around us. Some of my staff had gone ahead of my retinue and readied the castle for our arrival.

It was good to be back at Sárvár. I found the castle to be much warmer, and it felt a bit safer. The Turks receded and had not posed a threat to the region in recent years. My children loved to roam and play games within the halls of the castle. They were never allowed into the underground portion, but they kept occupied within the upper levels. I had brought in several tutors, one of which had been mine during my teenage confinement with Orsolya. The children would soon all be off to study at other castles and would only visit once or twice per year. I would miss them, but I knew having the advantage of education would benefit them, especially when they inherited the vast estates of Báthory-Nádasdy.

Darvulia brought in a new chambermaid for introductions. Her name was Teresa, and I found her to be very annoying.

"Greetings, Your Excellency! I look forward to serving you!" She beamed a wide, toothy smile at me.

"Teresa, I shall appoint you to assist Katalin with my morning routine. Please take note that I do not enjoy talking in the morning and prefer silence as I am readied."

"Yes, of course, my lady. I understand, some people

do not fare well in the mornings. I will take special care of you and make sure your day is started well."

I could not stand being near Teresa. Everything about her antagonized me, from the way she smiled to her enthusiastic demeanor and nasally voice. Darvulia chuckled as she steered the girl out of my proximity.

The next morning, Teresa woke me, several hours before my usual time to rise.

"It's a beautiful day outside, Your Excellency!" She threw open my draperies and opened the doors to allow the brisk cold air into my chambers.

"Who—what are you doing you insolent little bitch? Close the doors and draw my drapes! I do not rise before the hour of nine!" I startled Teresa with my fury and she closed the door and drapes quickly. "Now get out!" I reached for a candle holder and threw it at her, hitting her squarely in the back as she left my chambers.

I could not go back to sleep, which angered me more. I cherished sleep, and resented her for intruding on me. I was exhausted from my lack of sleep, irritated easily by the smallest of offenses. The other servants knew well enough to stay away.

Later that morning, Teresa returned, this time with Darvulia.

"Take care that you do not disturb me in the early hours of the morning!" I snapped.

"Yes, my lady. I did not expect Teresa to rouse you so early," Darvulia said.

"See that it does not happen again. Tie her up if you have to, but see that she does not disturb my sleep!"

"I apologize, my lady, please forgive me! Here, allow me to fasten your underpinnings," Teresa said happily. I growled but allowed her to apply my chemise and corset. She continued to chatter on about her childhood home in Buda, and some other blathering about her job in a castle there. Finally, I had enough of her and I grasped her by the throat.

"You will cease to speak this instant!"

"I'm so sorry—" I squeezed her neck harder and she tried to release my grasp with her fingernails. I slapped her and told Darvulia to tie her to the settee.

"Your Excellency, I will try harder to please you, I beg of you to release me!" Teresa cried.

I ignored her and called for Ficko. "Bring me a trimmer from the gardener's shed." He left and returned quickly bearing a rusted, jagged-toothed hand saw, made for trimming tree branches and shrubs.

"You shall never invade my psyche with your blithering ever again!" I took the saw and proceeded to rip apart Teresa's mouth. The more she struggled to move her head away, the more damage the saw did to her face. When I finished, she had fainted and would surely die soon from the loss of blood. Ficko removed Teresa from my chambers and Darvulia cleaned up the bloody mess.

"Do not think to bring another servant into my presence like that ever again!" I scolded Darvulia and left the room to wash the blood from my skin and change my clothes.

Darvulia did not approach me the rest of the day. The next evening, she brought me a gift that I had been wanting for some time. It was a lovely Venetian mirror. She knew me too well. It softened my mood as soon as I saw it.

She fastened it to my waist with a silk ribbon, and I gazed into it, admiring my face and hair. It was small and round, and it reflected a near-perfect image.

"I had this made for you, my lady, and I am happy

that it finally arrived from Venice this morning. May it please you." She curtsied. I held her and kissed her soft cheek.

"Thank you, it is beautiful."

"Not so beautiful as its owner."

I examined the mirror's case. It was made from the finest mahogany wood, carved with intricate leaves and flowers. I found myself looking at my image often, and I wore it always.

"How have you been since Ferencz's departure?" Darvulia asked.

"I am well, but a little depressed that I might not see him for some time."

"I have found a way you might be able to see him, my lady."

"How?" I asked eagerly.

"Tonight I will show you. I must collect a few herbs for a brew and I will return shortly.

When she came back, she had with her a cup of strong-smelling dark tea.

"What's in it?"

"Herbs that will set your mind free from your body and allow you to roam the universe while you are under its spell."

"I shall not die from it?"

"No, it's perfectly safe, but powerful."

I smelled it and turned away. "You expect me to drink this?"

"Yes, in order to travel to see Ferencz. It contains herbs of acacia, mugwort, belladonna, and basil, among other special spices."

"You are certain this will cause me no harm?"

"Yes, I'm certain. In small doses, these herbs blended together will send you on your voyage in flight. In large doses, they could kill a person, and you must not drink it often."

I drank the tea, swallowing it quickly so as not to taste it. Darvulia readied me for bed and she lay next to me. I stared up at my coat of arms above the doorway, and read my motto over and over, *"Contra naturum."* I felt as if I were floating and then falling back to earth. Softly, Darvulia spoke of Ferencz, until her voice fell away and I began to see his encampment with my mind's eye.

I walked through a field in the cold dark of night, through a mass of rotting corpses strewn around from the ravages of war. The fetid smell of decaying bodies rose to fill my nostrils and I hurried toward Ferencz's encampment.

I knew instinctively which tent was Ferencz's and walked in through the fabric wall. Ferencz stood tall and lean, his head almost touching the roof of his tent. He was alone and seemed depressed. I smelled the faint scent of hashish, and I could hear men talking outside of his tent. I stood near him, but he did not see me. I called to him, but he did not hear my voice. He lay on his bed, dark eyes wide open. I lay next to him and I could smell his musty scent and feel his body's warmth. How I longed to touch him in person, for him to feel my presence.

A guard brought in a prostitute and I stood to the side of his cot. She was foreign, with dark skin and black eyes, heavily lined with kohl. Her lips were thin but had been overstated with crimson gloss. I watched her disrobe to expose her tanned supple body to him. She moved to the end of his cot and lingered for a moment. Ferencz watched her, but seemed to stare past her. She crawled onto his cot with him and fellated him for a few minutes, leaving a ring of red gloss around his penis. His erection was bold and hard, but he wasn't enjoying himself, not the way he did when I pleasured him. The whore sat on his erection and he grunted and grasped her breasts as they bounced up and down with each movement and thrust.

I walked over to the cot and climbed on, melting my soul into the whore's existence. I had taken her body, and felt every inch of Ferencz inside of me. He recognized me quickly and I felt him grab my hair.

"My beauty, my wife, you are here! Oh my gods, I have longed for you..." He was lost in pleasure as I rode him, sucked his nipples and bit at his ear lobes. I could taste the salty tears that rolled down his cheeks.

When we were both spent, I did not move from his lap right away, but I knew the power of the potion was lessening.

"I must go soon, my love."

"No, no, stay with me. I do not know how you are able to do this, but please stay," he pleaded.

"This brew of herbs that Darvulia gave me will wear off soon, and I must be careful of how much I ingest. They are very powerful herbs."

"Do not bring harm to yourself, my love, please be careful." He held me tightly in his arms, but his embrace did not impede my soul's escape.

"I must take my leave now, please know that you are in my thoughts every moment. Come home soon," I rose and went to the side of the cot, watching him as he watched me. He did not notice the prostitute still sat atop his lap, and he reached for my spirit as it left the tent.

When I awoke, Darvulia was curled up beside me, peacefully on the edge of sleep. I had a fretful headache, but I willed my body to arise so that I could wash my face. I wondered if what had happened had been real. I noticed a trickle of fluid dripping down my leg, and I had a bruise where Ferencz had grabbed my breast.

"Did you enjoy your visit with your husband, my lady?" Darvulia said drowsily.

"Yes, it felt very real."

"It was real, in your heart, in your soul. I assure you, he felt you." I considered her words and watched for correspondence from him over the next month. He did not disappoint me.

> *My beloved wife,*
>
> *I am consumed with thoughts of you every day and every night. Your beautiful face haunts me and I long for you. Your presence in my mind keeps me moving forward in this war, knowing that I am fighting to protect you and our possessions. I dreamt that you visited me in my tent one night, and I begged the gods for it to be real. Was it real or had I been tricked by the demons of smoke and drink? I do not care, I only long for more.*
>
> *Your husband,*
> *Ferencz*

I reread the short letter several times. I wanted more of the tea, but Darvulia feared for my safety and would not give me the recipe.

"You must not abuse these herbs. Ferencz shall be home soon, and we want you to be alive and healthy upon his arrival," she chided me. Darvulia was the only servant I allowed to speak to me in such a manner.

She had interviewed and hired more female servants, all of whom fell short of my expectations. One afternoon, I was being prepared to receive Polish nobility and a small delegation from the Holy Roman Emperor, Rudolf. They wished to secure a loan from me—or rather from Ferencz—to further their cause against the Turks.

Darvulia dressed me in a sapphire blue gown, embroidered with flowers and acorns. My hair was braided and embellished carefully by Katalin.

My look was almost complete; the only thing I lacked was a starched white neck ruff and some jewelry.

"I will call for Lena, she is in charge of starching and shaping your ruffs, my lady," Katalin went to retrieve Lena while I chose my jewelry.

Lena, a frail girl, about sixteen, entered with my neck ruff. She had used irons on it, which she had brought with her and heated in my fireplace. As she placed the ruff around my neck, I noticed that it had been scorched.

"Did you see these burn marks on the lace, Lena?" I asked.

"No, my lady, I did not, I apologize. Here, allow me to turn it in this direction and maybe I will be able to conceal the marks."

Her sloppy work and offer to cover up her mess inflamed my temper. I grabbed a mitt and pulled the hot iron from the fireplace and beat her with it, scorching her skin as she had done to my ruff. The smell of her burned skin excited me, but before I could do more, she escaped my room and ran down the hall. I chased her with the hot iron, wanting to hear the sizzle of her skin and smell her burning flesh, but she had fled quickly, and I realized that I had to continue to prepare for the arrival of my noble guests.

"See that Lena is confined. I may wish to visit her after the guests retire," I yelled to Darvulia.

Hours later, I thought the dinner would never end. I had a servant show the delegation to their rooms, and I rushed off to find Darvulia. Darvulia brought Lena to my room and had her kneel before me. The girl had been beaten for running away, her face was bruised and swollen.

"You are a disobedient nave, and your work has been sloppy. Rumor also has it that you have been having an affair with one of my cooks? You are recently married, are you not?" I inquired.

"Yes, Mistress, I am married. My husband Kristóf is away at war," she mumbled through swollen lips.

"So while your valiant husband is away, you are off frolicking with other men?"

"I am ashamed of my behavior, Mistress. Please have mercy on me, I shall repent," she folded her hands and bowed her head in prayer.

"Unless you are praying to me, that course of action shall do you no good."

She looked up at me in shock. "I wish no blasphemy, Mistress. I owe my Lord and Savior my prayers of penitence."

The holy war between Martin Luther and the Catholics had made me weary. I did not care about religion, be it Catholic or Protestant, as long as it was anti-Turkish. Even through the hundreds of masses I attended, not once had I ever repented for anything I had felt or done. *Try walking in my shoes,* I thought to myself as I listened to priests drone on about repentance. Darvulia's paganism had interested me more, mainly because I saw the results of its power.

"No worries, you shall meet your savior soon enough. Darvulia, please escort this girl to the lower level and ready her for my arrival. I shall join you in a few moments."

"Yes, my lady," Darvulia took Lena's hand and practically dragged her to their destination below. After they left, I chose two irons from the laundry drawer and made my way to the dungeon where my prey nervously waited. When she saw me enter the dungeon, she shrieked in terror and tried to escape the table to which Darvulia had secured her.

"Steady, hold steady while we wait for these irons to heat." I threw the irons into the hot coals and smiled an evil grin at Lena. Darvulia secured a rag in Lena's mouth to muffle her screams.

I landed my whip across Lena's legs and then again across her shoulders and neck. Angry red marks marred her beautiful complexion. She writhed in pain, and tried to escape her bindings, but her efforts were futile. Her legs were spread wide for my inspection. I fingered her pudendum, admiring the light fuzz that covered it. Once the irons were hot, I donned a mitt and selected a narrow iron. Lena watched me and whimpered as I brought the iron closer to her genitalia.

"How was the cook when you took him? Was he well endowed?" I held the iron up and surveyed its length. It was much longer and narrower than a man, and when cold, it may have produced a pleasurable experience for its recipient.

I lightly ran the hot iron over Lena's delicate parts, first the lips and then her clitoris. I was wet with anticipation as the girl screamed against the muffle. With one swift movement, I shoved the iron up inside the girl and listened to the sizzle of cauterization. I rubbed my own parts as I delivered the punishment. In and out, stirring around and around, I moved the iron as a man would thrust himself into a woman. As I climaxed, Lena fainted from the agony of my torture. I left her for Ficko to finish off.

When the weather permitted, Ferencz came home for a visit, this time without Miklós. I could see he was withdrawn and in low spirits, and I gave him time before I approached him about his melancholy.

"What ails you, my lord?" I asked him softly as he lay on his bed.

"Miklós, my dear friend, my brother in arms, has passed on from this world."

"Oh dear gods, what happened?"

"He was killed by those filthy Turkish mongrels!" He paused, and I kept silent to allow him to continue. "We had fought side by side. Our garrison had held back hundreds of Turks, but one got through our forces and into our encampment. That bastard... He impaled Miklós and left him to rot on a stake, and then ran away like a coward. I hunted him down and when I caught him, I had the perfect torture ready." Ferencz stared straight ahead, picturing the demise of his enemy.

"What did you do?"

"I devised a cage from our hunting traps. We imbedded sharp blades on the interior of the device. We placed him inside, and then raised him into the air. He was like a caged animal inside my trap. There was no way out for him."

"And did you leave him inside the cage?" My curiosity grew about this contraption. I knew Ferencz was well known for his punishments on the field, and this one in particular interested me for my own uses.

"For a while, and then my guards and I played

a little game with him. We stabbed at him with our swords and hot pokers, forcing him to the sides of the cage and onto the blades, perforating his skin. His life force dripped from his body and he perished in the cage. After we quartered his parts, we fed him to the wolves."

"You must build me a cage for our dungeon. It will detour disobedience from the servants." Ferencz looked surprised at my request.

"Of course, my dear, I will have one made for you." He smiled and kissed my cheek, his mood brightened.

Eleven

A messenger arrived at the castle with news from Transylvania. My brother János was dead. I had not seen or heard from him since my wedding, when he was expected to travel to Wallachia to marry the daughter of the high treasurer. The engagement ended on a sour note when János's future father-in-law, Barto Antonescu, caught János copulating with his wife, János's future mother-in-law. Barto expelled János from the castle immediately, and from there, János turned to thievery. According to the message I received, János had been caught stealing money from a monastery. Prince Sigismund Báthory, our cousin, had János arrested and thrown into prison, where he spent his remaining days. My reaction to the news of his death was stoic; János was nothing to me, other than a terror in my youth. I had held no familial love in my heart for him. I threw down the letter and picked up a report on the Turkish invasions of Hungary.

Tireless in their pursuits of land and riches, the Turkish army grasped for whatever they could claim as their empire waxed and waned. Other countries, including Hungary, used alternate routes to import and export goods, and this action damaged the Ottoman economy. The Turks had their hands full with King Philip of Spain, the Persians and the Austrians, fighting over the lands of Europe and Asia. Each time they lost a region, the Turks bounced back quickly, and gained other lands. Sultan Murad enjoyed the fruits of his army's efforts, sealed away in his palace in Constantinople with a limitless supply of food and myriad of wives and concubines. He had sired over one hundred children, many of whom were killed after his death by Murad's successor and son, Mehmed.

Ferencz and I spent a great deal of time together, often discussing the Turks and his tours of duty.

"I wonder what it would be like to have over one hundred children running around the castle?" I joked.

"I wonder what it would be like to *make* all of those children." He grinned at me, and reached out to tickle my neck.

"The sultan has no respect for how powerful our forces are, combined with the armies of Transylvania."

"No, but he will have a good dose of our power thrust in his fat face soon enough. The emperor has new plans for him."

"How I would love to see him in our new cage, suspended from the ceiling," I mused.

"It couldn't hold his weight," Ferencz laughed, "and the poor servants would be cleaning up a mess of fat and gristle for weeks."

Since our new torture device had been completed, the servants had been careful, and feared for their lives. I had decided that fear alone should not be the driving force behind their allegiance to us. If a servant did well while in continuous service for five years and they had proved to be loyal, they were rewarded handsomely. I granted the men small parcels of land and supplies to build a meager household. To the women, I endowed a generous dowry and textiles.

Ferencz appreciated my efforts in running the estates smoothly. He did not like having to deal with household issues, and did not involve himself when he was home. Often, he would defer to my opinions on issues that arose, leaving the household decisions to me as I left the war to him.

I visited the local villages often. I liked to see for myself the temperament of the community before making plans to raise taxes. The revolt that had led to the deaths of my sisters was well burned into my mind and I did not want to lose control as my father had. He had rarely visited the people who supported our aristocracy, and I thought it was important to see first hand the workings of the local economy and gain the trust of the people.

After Ferencz left for his next war campaign, I took a small retinue into the local villages. I made a point of buying something from almost all of the tradesmen. I complimented them on their business efforts and showed my support of their work. I also took the opportunity to impress upon the townspeople that a good portion of the taxes and rents paid were used for their own protection. I felt it was important they know some of it went toward protecting our lands from the Turkish devils that Ferencz so faithfully fought in our honor. They remembered the last attack on the Sárvár region and were grateful to have such a fearsome fighter on their side.

On our way back to the castle, our carriage sped quickly on the path toward home, leaving a grand trail of dust behind. I looked out the window and admired the lovely Hungarian countryside. The colors and scents of wildflowers, coupled with the brilliant sunshine and brisk air made me feel jubilant. As I continued to take in the scenery, I saw a woman sitting by herself on the side of the path. Normally, I would not give much thought to a pauper's predicament, but this woman was no pauper. Dressed simply in a finely made silk gown with embroidered guards and lace ruffs, I could tell her rank was not of the lower classes.

"Halt the carriage, Ficko!" I stepped out as soon as the carriage stopped and I went over to the woman. Her dirty brown hair was whipped around her face by the afternoon wind. As carriages drove by, she was enveloped in clouds of dust from the path. She was covered in filth and grime. Her beautiful silk gown was ruined.

"Madam," I called to her, but she did not acknowledge me. My retinue stood nearby, assessing the potential of danger.

"Your Excellency, do take care," Darvulia called to me.

"Madam, I am Countess Báthory, mistress of these lands. I would like to know why you are seated here by yourself."

She finally looked over at me, and tears started to fall from her large blue eyes. "I beg your pardon, Your Excellency, for I cannot rise to acknowledge you. Should I stand, I think I might faint."

"It is of no concern to me at this moment, my lady. What is your name?" I went over to her side and sat next to her.

"I am Margit Gáspár, I am… was a textile merchant's wife."

"You are the wife of Jakab Gáspár, are you not?"

"Yes he was my husband, but no more."

"Why are you here? Should you not be home with him?"

"He has thrown me out of my own home and has taken a new younger woman as his companion."

Margit was not young, but she was not decrepit or ugly. I knew her husband well, as he supplied my seamstresses with some of the finest fabrics for my gowns and livery.

"You are out on the streets, without food or shelter, because of your husband's lust for a younger woman?"

"Yes, my lady. We were together for over fifteen years. In that time, I could not bear him children. He felt that was reason enough to cast me out. He even gave her all of my fine gowns and personal items. I have nothing but the clothes on my back. I have no family here, and since my exile from my home, none of our neighbors or friends will acknowledge me."

"This is an outrage! You will accompany me back to Castle Sárvár." I knew that this sort of thing happened everyday, but seeing this woman destitute, and knowing that a younger prettier woman had taken over her household and belongings, infuriated me. I pictured myself in this woman's quandary and it made my blood boil.

"You are most generous, but I do not wish to be a burden."

"It is my pleasure to assist you, dear lady." During our ride, I studied the woman. She fell asleep in her seat across from me. I could tell her skin had been fine in her youth, and it was marred by only a few lines of age. Her brown hair was lightly streaked with gray, and she was not overly heavy in stature. I could not understand why a husband of over fifteen years would throw out a faithful wife.

Ferencz and I had been married over twenty years, and we still loved each other fiercely and passionately. I touched my face and felt my own lines of age. I pulled out my looking glass and surveyed my hair; my maids had always done a fine job coloring it, and I was relieved to see no weeds of gray within my thick mass of locks. My figure was svelte, although my breasts had sagged a bit from childbearing.

I kept imagining myself a dirty heap on the side of the road, cast away by Ferencz. I imagined a teenage chambermaid taking over my fine gowns and cosmetics, my staff becoming loyal to her. My fury was rising as I worried. Darvulia must have sensed my anxiety.

"No worries, my lady. You have borne Ferencz several healthy children, you manage his estates better than he could ever endeavor, and you are beautiful and well thought of throughout Hungary. Ferencz would never cast you aside."

I could not answer her compliments. I knew all of these things to be true, but Margit's presence brought forward the reality of things. Men often preferred young girls to their faithful wives. A wife could do her duty and serve her husband and then find herself used up and cast out.

When we arrived at Castle Sárvár, I could see Margit was in awe of the estate.

"Darvulia, please see that Margit is well bathed and refreshed with food and drink. Install her in the south tower suite of rooms. I will send over Katalin with some of my gowns, along with the seamstresses for fittings."

"Oh, Your Excellency, you are most kind, thank you." She lowered her head and fell into a deep curtsy.

I brought her up to face me, "Let me know if you

have need of anything."

For the next several weeks, the sight of my young chambermaids irritated me, and they suffered greatly from my malicious mood. I had Ficko bring me a branding iron from the stables. I used it whenever the desire struck me, stamping the Báthory-Nádasdy brand on the backsides, faces and limbs of any young girl who happened to be in my presence at the wrong time. Much to the enjoyment of the male servants, I forced many of the young girls to do their chores in the nude, so that I could torture them more easily. Deep were my cravings to gaze at them, but at the same time I hated seeing how perfect they all were. Just looking at their beautiful hair and nubile young bodies with their youthful breasts, so taut and supple, taunted my psyche. I dragged one young girl by the hair into the herb garden and threw her slender naked body into a bush of stinging nettles. The sight of youthful creamy skin made my mouth water, and I would bite and chew the flesh of any young servant girl that incited my anger. My temper flared like a rabid animal, and nothing could placate my rage.

"Darvulia, every female servant under the age of thirty shall be completely shorn of all hair," I ordered. I wanted to erase all of their beauty.

"Yes, my lady." Darvulia knew better than to question me while I was on a rampage.

She set to work immediately. There was little protest as the servants were reminded of the cage in the dungeon I had aptly named the Hanging Cage. Piles of hair were collected in bunches, organized by color and brought to me. I ran my fingers over the soft collection of tresses and laughed to myself, but I wasn't even close to being finished.

"Ficko, bring me Jakab Gáspár's new concubine.

Do not tell her that I am calling for her attendance, but bring her here somehow, without drawing attention."

"Yes, my lady."

Ficko returned late that evening with Jeselle Gáspár, bound and gagged and rolled up in a sack, which he laid at my feet. I could see her movements through the cloth bag.

"Did anyone see you?"

"No my lady, the household was asleep. I stole into her window and took her from her bed," he said in his slurred voice.

"Excellent work, Ficko. You will be rewarded. Take her to the dungeon and install her in the Hanging Cage."

I followed behind Ficko as he dragged Jeselle to the dungeon. He had bound her well and she was unable to struggle much. When he ripped open the bag, she stared straight up at me. She was a lovely blonde woman with a delicately featured face. Her nose was small and slightly turned up at the end, her large green eyes and fair skin gave away her Nordic heritage.

She looked from me to the iron cage and cried, muffled through her gag, "No! No, please don't hurt me!"

I punched her hard, several times, until she passed out. Ficko cut her bindings and removed her clothing. He lowered the cage and placed her inside of it, and then raised the cage back into the air.

The cage was made of shiny black strips of metal, and the interior was lined with razor-sharp blades. It was suspended in the air by heavy metal chains, which creaked and rattled when the cage was raised or lowered. Ferencz had Derosh build two thrones beneath the cage, so that we could view our captives without obstruction. They were too far away for my enjoyment, so I stood directly beneath the cage. When Jeselle awoke, I had a long hot poker waiting for her. I stabbed at her and burned her bare feet with the poker.

"Stop, you crazy animal! Stop! I don't know who you are but you had best release me now!"

A throaty laugh escaped me as I reminded her of her situation, "I don't think you realize that you are in no position to be giving out orders, dear girl." I proceeded to poke at her from below. I stepped out of the way as she started to wet herself.

"Let me go, you savage! I demand to be set free!" she screamed at the top of her lungs. Her pale face became red and blotchy with anger.

"I am Countess Báthory, and you are here to appease my displeasure with your relationship with Jakab Gáspár."

The girl looked stunned. "What does Jakab have to do with this? Do you want money to release me? He will pay anything for my release."

"No, I do not want your husband's money you stupid little shit! I want you to die a horrible, painful death, just because you exist." I sunk the hot poker into her long, beautifully shaped leg and she screamed in agony.

I threw down the poker and observed Jeselle. She lay at the bottom of the cage and I grabbed her long blonde hair and pulled. I swung from her long locks; her screams were like music to my mind. I jumped down from my swing and she stood upright. I rocked the cage with the poker, and she fell into the piercing blades.

Her skin was sliced into ribbons and blood dripped from her wounds. I tore the sleeves from my gown and ripped open my bodice and then stood under the cage as her blood rained down on me. I relished its warmth and stickiness, and rubbed it into the skin of my arms, my breasts, my neck and face. My mind ticked away with visions of stealing Jeselle's beauty and youth by absorbing her blood. *Yes, it had to be possible. The apothecary had told me there were many uses for fresh blood.*

Darvulia walked in and stifled back a scream. I was soaked from head to toe in Jeselle's blood. She lay above me in the cage, dead from her blood loss. Shaking her head, Darvulia approached me with tears in her eyes.

"My lady, let me strip you of these soiled clothes and get you into a bath." I allowed her to remove the gown and led me to my chambers for a bath. She added soothing oils and milk to the bath and helped me step in.

Darvulia worked up a lather of bubbles and washed my thick hair. She gently scrubbed the bloodstains from my skin, and when I was clean, she had me lay on my bed for the appliance of oil essences. My skin felt warm and alive. Darvulia left me to rest, but I got up and examined myself in the large full-length Venetian mirror within my wardrobe. I ran my fingers over my skin and felt its softness. It had been revitalized. I could not attribute this to the oils alone, as Darvulia massaged me with them often enough. My skin had consumed Jeselle's beauty.

The next morning, the village was astir with the news of Jeselle's disappearance. Following my orders, Ficko buried the girl in a shallow grave on the outskirts of town. He then spread a rumor at a local tavern that Jeselle had probably left Jakab because he was an old useless boar, and that she had likely stolen his money.

The rumor spread like wildfire and soon, everyone had their own opinions of Jakab and the poor treatment of his first wife, Margit. People said that Jakab had killed Jeselle himself and buried her in the forest.

The news of Jeselle's disappearance reached Margit quickly. I had Ficko, a priest, and my notary accompany her to her old home to remove what was rightfully hers, and to deliver a formal decree of divorce on the grounds of adultery and abandonment. I had pulled in many favors from the court of the Holy Roman Emperor to obtain her divorce. When she returned, she was aglow.

"Thank you, dear lady, for all of your help. I now have all of my beautiful things, and I am free of the adulterer. How can I ever repay you?" she asked humbly, her eyes filled with gratitude.

"Well, you could start by overseeing my estate, Castle Poszóny." I smiled at her.

My request caught her off guard. "It would be an honor, Your Excellency." she curtsied low.

"It shall be done. My staff will transport you and your belongings, and whatever else you might need tomorrow morning. My notary and his staff will be sent to teach you all you will need to know about managing the estate. I shall visit soon to see your progress. If you do well, I will reward you generously."

Alone and destitute no more, Margit held her head high and was joyfully installed at Poszóny for many years to come.

I sent my daughter Katalin to assist Margit and learn the duties of running the castle together.

Katalin would be of great help to Margit as I had already taught her much about managing an estate. She would soon be married, so the experience with Margit would fortify my teachings.

I had arranged for Katalin to be engaged to one of my half-brother's sons, Count György Drugét de Homonna. My mother Anna had been married and widowed twice before she married her cousin, my father. With her first husband, Baron Gáspár Drafgi, she gave birth to my brother János. After Gáspár's death, she married the wealthy Count Antal Drugét de Homonna, who was a distant relative of Marguerite de Valois and the Medici family. I could only hope that Katalin's marriage to György would be as much of a blessing as mine had been to Ferencz.

Twelve

hen Ferencz returned from his tour of duty, he did not comment when a nearly-bald laundress tended to his clothing. I allowed the girls to dress and their hair to grow back, but my jealousy and rage for their youth boiled beneath still waters.

"You seem a bit stressed, my dear. I propose we go on a trip to Vienna this summer. It will be relaxing to get away together, and the emperor has offered one of his palaces there to use. There is much that I would like to show you," he said as he changed into a more comfortable set of robes.

"I would love to go to Vienna with you, but you just arrived back from war, do you not want to rest for a short while?"

"For a short while, yes, but I want to take a very small retinue and steal you away from our castle for a break."

"Very well, we shall go at your leisure, my lord."

"There are so many new things in Vienna that you have not seen. Your trunks will be full of many beautiful types of finery on our return, and you will be pampered. There is also a torture device there from

Nuremberg that will interest you."

"This respite is sounding more and more appealing, dear husband. I shall look forward to it." I could almost picture the trunks of fine fabrics, jewels and perfumes I would acquire. "Tell me of this torture device."

"I believe the emperor called it an Iron Virgin. It works with the gears of a clock. The victim stands before it, and the arms of this woman-shaped device holds him and brings him inside. As her arms close, spikes penetrate through the victim's body, ultimately crushing him."

"Fascinating, I would like to see it work." I was eager to learn more about this new torture device, but Ferencz was more interested in my plans for the evening, and of course, food.

"Did I hear that you have some entertainment planned for this evening's feast?"

"Yes, I have invited an orchestra from the eastern region to entertain us while we dine tonight."

"You always know how to soothe me after a tour of duty. I shall see you at dinner then, my love." He kissed me tenderly and I jumped down from his bed and left his chambers.

The orchestra had arrived at Sárvár a few weeks before Ferencz arrived home. There were lutes, vielles, wind whistles, horns and a harp, as well as a percussionist.

I made sure the cooks were well-stocked with imported spices, a fresh slaughter of meats, herbs and vegetables. The dining hall was alight with candles and torchlight, and the heavenly smells of food drifted around us. The musicians played quietly as the servers delivered our food, fast on their feet, and without flaw.

I took a deep drink of wine and sat back to take

in the music. It soothed my nerves, and I could tell Ferencz enjoyed it as well.

"We should have music with dinner every night," he mused.

"Yes, we should, I shall see what I can do about that." I smiled at him. After dinner, I spoke to the lead musician. His name was Andrei, and he was a decrepit old man with leather-like skin and white hair. He was a flautist, and had long, well manicured fingers.

"Lord Andrei, a word with you for a moment."

"Yes, Your Excellency." His tired, watery blue eyes turned brighter.

"We are very pleased with your group's performance this evening."

"Thank you, my lady, I am happy that it pleased you." He bowed a low bow, and I feared he would not be able to rise, but he managed to return to meet my gaze.

"We would like to see you here at the castle more often. I offer your faction a permanent place within our household."

"Oh, my lady, that is very generous, yes indeed, but I will need to consult with the other members before I agree. There are some of us with families who await our return."

"Please do consider the offer, as it would displease us greatly should you decline," I warned him gently.

Andrei left to speak with the other musicians and then came back alone, his stature slouched.

"I am sorry to report, my lady, that we will be unable to accept your kind offer. My regrets." He bowed again.

"This is most displeasing," I told him as I stroked my chin. I motioned for the servants to close the doors and leave the dining hall. "Play for us again." I directed the musicians to sit down and play more.

"We were just putting our instruments away, Your Excellency, perhaps tomorrow before we leave we could play for you again."

"No, now. I require it. Be seated and play again." He backed away and discussed the situation with the other players. Ferencz was still seated, drinking wine and carrying on with his troops who had joined us for dinner. He was oblivious to any problems with the musicians.

"My lady," Andrei had returned, "I must beg your pardon tonight, but we are unable to play longer this evening."

"No, you will play for us until I tell you it is time to stop." I motioned for two guards to come over. "Tie these men to their seats." The guards grabbed Andrei and dragged him over to his seat. The other players were shocked, but they willingly sat down. All nine members of the orchestra were tied to their seats at the waist and feet, and then were handed their instruments.

"My lady, this is most appalling, please release us," Andrei implored.

"Play. I care not what as long as it is pleasing to hear. Do not stop until I order you to stop," I commanded. The guards stood closely behind the orchestra, hands near their swords.

The orchestra played for two more hours without a break. Ferencz had not noticed that they were tied to their seats, and he continued to drink and socialize with his guests. By the time Ferencz chose to retire, many of the players' fingers were bleeding.

"Guards, escort these men to their accommodations." They were taken to their rooms and locked away for several days. I ordered them to play again. In protest, none of the men had eaten, so I had Ficko and two guards beat them into submission.

When they were brought to play again, they wearily took their seats, picked up their instruments and began to play.

Ferencz got up and clapped his hands. "I am tired of these soft vignettes, play something with fervor! I want to dance with my wife!" He took my hand and led me into an energetic dance. I looked back at Andrei, who in turn, stared back at me with daggers. I smiled and continued to enjoy myself with Ferencz.

When the evening's festivities ended, the players looked to me for the order to cease playing. I nodded and they were escorted to their chambers and locked away. The next morning, Darvulia approached me.

"Dear lady, Andrei the musician requests an audience with you. Shall I send for him?"

"Yes, very well."

Andrei was brought in and stood before me. I fingered the jewels on my gilded throne and looked at him.

"Speak, Andrei."

"Madam, I beg you to allow us to leave."

"I have quite enjoyed your music, why should I allow you to leave?" I said, capriciously.

"With all due respect, you cannot force a caged bird to sing."

I thought for a moment and responded, "I can."

"Madam, please, I am begging you to allow us to leave, if not me, then please allow my three youngest members to return to their wives and children."

"The group would not be the same without you all. We would not be pleased if you did not provide the same quality of music each night."

Andrei dropped to his knees and began to cry. Much

to my surprise, he rose and charged at me as I sat on my throne. He tore away my fine white ruff and his long fingers found their way around my slender neck, pressing and squeezing the breath out of my body. I felt my eyes bulge as I was choking. Our struggle was so fierce, we tipped over my throne, his grip never loosened.

Ficko jumped in and tried to pry him off of me, but he was unable to free me from Andrei's grasp. My will to live was strong, and with one last surge of power, I thrust my knee into his groin which sent him down, writhing in pain. I pulled away from him, reeling in shock over the struggle. Ficko brought in the guards, and Darvulia raced over to my side.

"My lady, let me attend to you." She examined my neck and body. I was bruised and unable to speak for several days, but my ego was more damaged than my person.

Ferencz made sure that Andrei and his musicians did not fare well. When he found out what had happened, he was livid with rage. They were all taken to the dungeon, caged without food or water, and beaten several times per day. When I regained my strength and my voice, Ferencz and I delivered their final punishment.

"Are you well now, my love?" Ferencz asked with much tenderness.

"Yes, just a few bruises, but I am fine."

"These men shall pay with their lives for this transgression. No man is entitled to touch your body, much less bruise it." Anger flared in his dark eyes as he spoke.

Derosh lowered the Hanging Cage and opened the door. Each of the nine men were brought forth and installed in the cage, one at a time. Andrei would be the last, as Ferencz thought it fitting that he should watch as his entire group was killed. Andrei cried as he saw each man die inside the cage.

Ferencz and I were seated on our thrones hand in hand, no different than we would have been if we were watching a play or some other form of entertainment. When it was Andrei's turn, he looked around. The bodies of his group lay punctured and bloody. He was docile as he was placed inside and the heavy cage door shut.

"Finally, I have my caged bird before me," I jested up at Andrei. I nodded to Ficko to pull and turn the cage, throwing Andrei off balance and into the blades of death.

Ferencz and I left for Vienna in the spring as soon as the route to the north was passable. We stopped at Castle Poszóny and observed that Margit had been doing well in her job as overseer. In addition to a handsome salary for the year, I left her some of my old gowns, since I knew I would be buying fabric for new gowns in Vienna. I would no longer be purchasing textiles through Jakab Gáspár. He had been arrested for Jeselle's murder when the constable found her body in her shallow forest grave.

Ferencz and I had a brief but enjoyable visit with our daughter, Katalin. She had grown into a lovely young girl, graceful in her mannerisms and well-educated. She had Ferencz's wavy raven hair and dark piercing eyes. We discussed her future wedding plans. I thought Ferencz would be bored listening to us chatter, but he joined in as we made arrangements.

After our visit at Poszóny, our final destination was Katterburg Palace, a vast estate maintained by the emperor as a hunting reserve. Forested hills and meadows surrounded the sprawling palace, which boasted an enormous wine cellar and spacious marble bath house. I was enamored of the bath house and spent many hours in the hot rich mud and Grecian tubs that were fed by nearby mineral springs. Servants were always at the ready when I requested to be massaged, and there were also elaborate treatments for my hair which made it glisten in the sunshine.

Ferencz smiled each time I was off to indulge in a relaxing treatment, and often joined me in the hot baths. Besides being as relaxed and sated by the warmth and comfort of the waters, we also sated each other with passionate sex. We had been married over twenty years and the lovemaking never ceased to amaze me. I believed that Ferencz's time away at war had been good for our marriage; it had kept us hungry for one another. To be reunited each time he returned was like being with him for the first time. Hours of discovery, seduction, and primitive satisfaction filled almost every night of our retreat to Vienna.

One morning, we rose to soak in one of the mineral baths together. Blissfully naked, we relaxed in the soothing waters.

"I see you're enjoying the mineral baths. They look like they've done you a world of good, Sir Ferencz," Emperor Rudolf stood above us, after silently entering. He was dressed in brown velvet hose, tall black boots and a russet colored doublet. He chose to stand directly across from me, my breasts fully showing above the water. My face turned crimson, but I stayed in the water with Ferencz.

"Yes, Your Highness, thank you very much for this respite. I will be fully energized after this retreat," Ferencz replied, unaware of my embarrassment.

"I see that your lovely wife is also enjoying the waters." He peered at me with the lustful look of a mountain wolf. Time had not been kind to him over the years. I remembered him as a handsome young man when he attended our wedding. His face was drawn with many lines of age and his nose looked as if it had been broken once or twice. He snorted quite a bit, as if he had an ailment. The snorting grew annoying as did his presence.

"Yes, Your Highness, I am thankful for the opportunity to visit your palace grounds." I bowed my head and wished for him to leave. Normally, I was not ashamed of my body; male and female servants had always milled around me in every condition of dress or undress. But none of them ever looked at me in the unexplainable way Emperor Rudolf looked at me that morning. I felt violated after his gaze shifted back to Ferencz.

Ferencz stepped out of the water, wrapped himself in a plush robe and walked out talking business with the emperor. Later on, Ferencz reported back that the emperor requested our presence that evening at Castle Schönbühel, just outside of Vienna.

"It will be a grand feast, with much of the upper nobility of Europe to be in attendance. Wear your finest gown, I wish to show you off." He smiled jubilantly.

"I look forward to the evening. I hope that my maidservants can ready me quickly enough. It must be easy for you to throw on some slops and a doublet and you are ready," I teased him.

"Yes, it is a bit less complicated than for you." He grinned.

Darvulia and my servant girls worked fast, and dressed me in an exquisite French gown of emerald brocade. It was a beautiful contrast to my reddish hair, which had been upswept in a mass of curls and set with my pearl and emerald coronet. My skin was soft from the many weeks of bath treatments. Darvulia put the finishing touches on my makeup and dabbed the oil of cypress on my pulse points. When Ferencz saw me, he knelt down in front of me.

"I am love-struck by my beautiful bride," he said as he kissed my hand.

When we arrived, the event was already in full swing. There were several hundred people dining, conversing, and dancing to French and English style music. We were directed to sit at the high table with Emperor Rudolf. I felt my face turn red when he greeted us.

"Good evening, Countess, it is a pleasure to see you. I would be most happy if you would save a dance for me later on." He took my hand in his.

"Of course, Your Highness." I curtsied and slipped my hand from his grasp. Ferencz was oblivious to my uneasiness around the emperor.

"There are many new dances to learn tonight, Erzsébet, I think we will have an exciting evening," Ferencz said, as we watched people dance in perfect rhythm to the music.

"Yes, this will be most entertaining."

I sat in awe of the feast hall as I waited for the servants to bring me wine and food. The marble staircase and inlaid marble floors put Sárvár to shame. The high ceilings were ornate with religious scenes painted with brilliant colors. Cherubs and gargoyles were perched in every corner. The windows were covered in plush velvet fabrics, and the furniture in the main foyer was equally opulent.

When my wine arrived, I sat and watched a few dozen couples dance. People from every part of Europe were in attendance, enjoying themselves over the food, wine and music. The music's pace changed often, from slow to fast, each couple keeping in perfect step. Hungarian music was folkish and unrefined compared to the English and French pieces being played.

Women swirled around in gowns made from some of the finest fabrics, dyed in brilliant colors. Many wore large farthingales, hip padding and overstated ruffs. The men were dressed just as flamboyantly in their silken hose, paned slops and overstuffed doublets.

"Shall we dance?" asked Ferencz.

"Yes, I would love to. I hope I can keep up."

"Not to worry, the next is a pavane."

The music was slow and steady, two steps forward and one step back, circling left and swirling right, couples danced hand in hand in a decorous sweep all the way around the dance floor.

The next dance was the galliard, danced by only a few couples. It was a lively dance of embellished and complex variations of steps, lifts and jumps. The men who danced showed off their fine muscular legs and looked to be pleased with themselves for their energetic acrobatics.

My favorite dance was the branle, where almost everyone joined in, including Emperor Rudolf. *Good,* I thought, *this shall be his only dance with me.* The lively music led all the couples side to side, with hops and turns.

"This is so much fun, but I must stop. I am exhausted my love," I told Ferencz.

"I'm glad you're having a good time. Wait until tomorrow, I'm taking you shopping," Ferencz said.

"I hope I can move after all of this activity tonight."

"I'll keep you limber tonight." He winked at me.

True to his promise, we made love most of the night.

The next morning, we were off to the markets of Vienna. We stopped at a jeweler's shop where Ferencz bought me a cache of rings, necklaces and earrings, as well as many loose stones for embellishing my gowns. We then stopped at a textile merchant's shop, where I chose enough lengths of fabric for over ten gowns. The bill did not bother Ferencz in the least, so we kept shopping. I found some spicy ginger-scented perfume, imported from the Far East, and an ornate cedar trunk for Ferencz, as well as some silken hose that felt like a dream against my skin.

Our carriage was full of the day's treasures when we went back to Katterburg. I had the staff send most of the items to Sárvár, so that we would not be laden with finery, an easy target for thieves while traveling.

After we had returned to the palace, Ferencz decided he would like to rest before we dined that evening. He went back to his chambers to take a short nap. I dallied in the gardens, picking some lovely herbs and flowers. As I was coming in, I heard a loud crashing noise and Ferencz was swearing at someone.

"You miserable little thief!" Ferencz's voice rose. He threw a small end table at someone huddled on the floor nearby. "I've caught you stealing from me, which you will regret dearly."

Across the room, cowering in the corner was a servant boy staring up at Ferencz with large black eyes full of fear. He was Radu, a ten year-old orphan from Moldavia. The emperor had taken him in a few months before our visit. I noticed a few things of value had been missing, but I didn't think much of it at the time. At Ferencz's feet lay a chest full of jewelry—rings that belonged to Ferencz along with a pile of my own jewels. A length of silk fabric and a small wooden container of hashish that Ferencz liked to keep in his chambers were beneath the jewels.

Ferencz stomped over and beat Radu with his bare hands. He picked up the boy and threw him across the room like a rag doll. The palace guards came in and took Radu away to the dungeon. Ferencz and I followed.

"We do not tolerate theft by any of the staff in this palace," the palace steward reassured Ferencz. "He will be dealt with expeditiously."

"I want to be the one to administer the punishment. Do you have any objections?" Ferencz asked.

"No, none at all. We will use whatever punishment you see fit to deliver as an example to the other servants."

Ferencz growled at the boy, who sat shaking in the corner of the cell. An hour later, a spit was made ready in the courtyard. All of the staff were called to order.

"Watch, listen and learn. This boy was caught stealing from our guests—guests of His Highness, Emperor Rudolf. This activity will not be tolerated, let this be a lesson to you all." The steward had Radu brought up into the courtyard. His body was then tied to a narrow metal rack, which the guards lifted and placed on the spit.

Radu screamed and struggled as the guards lit the fire and began to turn the spit, roasting him over the flames.

Ferencz stoked the fire and threw another log onto it for good measure. As Ferencz started to walk away, he spat on the boy, which made a sizzling sound as it hit his burning skin.

The smells of flesh cooking and hair burning were overpowering. Many of the servants turned their heads, and some cried as they watched Radu die a horrific death. Ferencz took my hand and we went back into the palace.

I bathed in the bath house, trying hard to remove the smell of the burning boy trapped in my nostrils. I discarded the surcoat that I had worn that day and put the scene of death and the sounds of Radu's screams out of my mind.

Thirteen

e stayed in Vienna for a year, and then made our way back to Castle Poszóny for Katalin's wedding. We arrived back at Sárvár at the end of September the following year, just before Ferencz's forty-seventh birthday. It had been a relaxing retreat to Vienna, but I was glad to be back at Sárvár. Ferencz did not want a birthday celebration or any special attention. I had planned a simple dinner in our chambers, along with some of the gifts I had purchased for him in Vienna. It was a simple, somber birthday.

"I'm feeling old, Erzsébet. Every year I go away to battle, I can feel age in my bones. My mind is still sharp, but my body does not move as it used to."

"I understand. The ravages of time are not kind. I have done everything one can possibly do to avoid growing old," I told him.

"But you look beautiful, as young as the first day I laid eyes upon you. You never seem to change. Me, on the other hand, I am a servant of war, and it shows on my hide."

"Maybe you should have spent more days in the baths with me at Katterburg," I teased him.

"I did spend time with you in the baths. I think that's what made me feel my age. I'm not used to such pampering. My body expects to sleep on a cold cot out in the middle of nowhere. My muscles expect to be tested and stretched to their limits. Do you realize that I haven't picked up a sword since before we left for Vienna?"

"I will have some of the armory stewards give you some practice if you'd like."

"Yes, I'll need it before I go back on tour in the spring."

"The emperor still expects you to fight?"

"He does not expect me to be out in the same capacity as I have been, but more of an advisor." He looked pensive as he studied the frescoes on the walls. There were religious scenes, commissioned by Orsolya while she was still alive, as well as scenes of Ferencz in triumph at war, standing encircled by bloodshed. His figure was illustrated wearing his signature black armor, inlaid with our coat of arms.

"I should think the emperor would allow you to retire from war soon."

"He thinks my skills and strategies are too valuable. I agreed to go back this spring, but I will request retirement at the end of the summer."

Ferencz left for his tour of duty as advisor to the emperor. I knew that he would not be able to resist the lure of battle, and as I predicted, a report was delivered that said Ferencz had led the forces in fighting off the Turks as they tried to take over the village of Győr. They had burned the village to the ground during the time Ferencz's father, Tamas, had defended it. This time, the Turks had no success and were beaten, burned and stabbed into submission.

Ferencz's recent birthday reminded me of my

own age. I would be forty-two years old, and many changes had been happening in my body. My fits of falling sickness had lessened, but my mind seemed to always be spinning strange thoughts. My moods were turbulent, and I suffered from numerous headaches that hurt so much I could not stand.

One afternoon, I went into a fit of rage and broke every mirror in the household. With a jolt of energy surging through my body, I ripped down the heavy glasses from the walls, and crushed them with an axe I found in the gardener's shed. As I stood amongst the shards of Venetian glass, I could see a distorted image of myself. I stood in the same spot for over an hour, observing myself in the shards from every angle. A brown eye here. A chin there. Long fingers grasping the axe in another pane. It was a plethora of freakish images of my body broken into a million pieces.

My ever-faithful servant Darvulia had always taken great care of me, and usually knew how to shake my melancholy moods. She had all of the young chambermaids shorn again, which brought a hearty laugh from my lips, but it did not banish my sense of becoming old.

I sent for my alchemist, Péter. Péter was a prolific student of science. I had known him in my youth, and had always valued his opinions on health and science. He had an open invitation at Sárvár, and was often found using the printing presses for publications of scientific documents.

"Péter, do you think there is an elixir for old age?" I asked him pointedly one morning.

"I believe that there is a potion to halt the process of aging, though there are many arguments against the validity of such thoughts."

I regarded Péter for a moment as he spoke. He was

forty years old, athletic, with dark hair and hazel eyes. He was in perfect physical condition and showed no lines of age on his face.

"You must have some answers that are valid, as you are near the same age as I am, and you show very little proof of time's grasp upon your body."

"Men age differently than women, my lady. We are made differently by our creator."

I snorted at the thought of a male god forming his male human counterpart to stay young and perfect, and then using the leftover refuse to make the female companion.

"I want you to make me a potion to stay young. I want something for my skin, for my joints, for my mind. I do not ever want to grow old." I thought of my mother in her condition before she died. I did not want to find myself in that condition, ever.

"I cannot guarantee any one mixture. We can try several things, until we find something that is right for you." I could hear the coins clinking in his mind, as I knew he would want payment for each concoction.

"Very well, then, return to me when you have something."

It took Péter three days to mix a potion of herbs and mineral water for me to drink and bathe in. A few days later, he brought me a poultice, said to have been used by the queen of England, made with herbs, egg whites, lead and vinegar to smooth into my skin. I liked the effect it had on my coloring, but I could still see lines on my face. He brought me lemon and rose water tea, a facial peel of mercury, alum, honey and eggshells, and various other mixtures, but none of them satisfied my needs.

"There may be other things that help, such as relieving any carnal urges you might have regularly, or have you tried regular mineral baths?" he asked, and I ignored him.

"What about blood?" I asked, thinking about my interlude with Jeselle Gáspár.

"I suppose there are many uses for blood, but it would have to be of the purest quality." Péter stroked his short beard as he thought about my proposal of a new ingredient.

"The blood of a beautiful girl, one that is pure and untouched."

"Blood coagulates quickly. It would have to be mixed with something else in order to maintain the proper consistency."

"Fine, then see to mixing a special potion for me. I shall bring you a cup of blood from one of my subjects this evening."

Later, I had Darvulia bring me one of my servant girls. I told her to pick the most beautiful of the young girls, a virgin preferably. She brought me a young girl named Zsofia. She was a stunning red haired girl, with a nubile young body and taut skin. *Yes,* I thought to myself, *I want some of her.* I circled around Zsofia after tearing off her clothes. She had a scared look in her eyes, and shivered with fear as I surveyed her body.

"She will do perfectly. You know what to do."

Darvulia returned later with a full chalice of blood. Ficko was told to bury Zsofia's remains in the forest.

Péter returned to my suite. "Here's the blood, I hope to see a potion in the morning," I told Péter as I handed him the chalice of blood. He looked surprised, but took the cup.

"I will see what I can do, and will visit in the morning," he said as he bowed and returned to his chambers.

The next morning, he brought a thin, dark, red

liquid to my chambers.

"Paint this over her entire body," Péter instructed Darvulia, "and apply olive oil afterwards and then rinse thoroughly."

I could not get rid of him fast enough, as I grabbed the potion and ran into my bathing area, Darvulia in tow.

"Paint me with this immediately," I ordered her. She found a brush and began the task of painting my skin with the blood mixture. As my skin was tickled by the brush's fine bristles, I imagined myself an image coming to life within a fresco. My pale skin absorbed every drop of the deep red solution. When Darvulia was finished, she massaged olive oil into my skin, and then rinsed my body. The solution did not stain my skin as the pure blood had done. The opposite had happened. My skin glowed, radiantly.

I was enamored of my skin's new vivacity, and used the mixture everyday. I felt younger, and decided to act younger. I grew tired of staring at the same old walls of Sárvár, day after day, waiting for Ferencz's return. I traveled with a small retinue to estates all over Hungary. I took Péter's advice about satisfying my carnal urges, and I had intercourse with several men as I visited different cities. I visited my Aunt Klára and her husband Antal Losonci. During my stay, I was exposed to Klára's deviant sexual experimentations.

Klára was my father's sister, the product of an affair their mother had with one of their uncles. She was rebellious, and always bucked against the morals and expectations of the Church. She was once seen wandering nude through Ecsed, howling up at a full moon like a mountain wolf. She had a malicious temper, and liked to torture and molest young girls and boys for her amusement. She would prostitute the children to soldiers when she had no further use for them. I found her to be entertaining, and I considered our visits educational as I always learned something new and licentious.

On our way home, Darvulia and I took in two German girls one night. They were walking through the forest and stumbled upon our encampment. Pliant and willing to please, they entertained us for several hours. When we finished with them, I had Darvulia extract blood from both girls to bring back to Péter upon our return to Sárvár. The blood could not be saved, much to my dismay, even though I had gone through great pains to preserve it.

"It has to be fresh in order to produce the correct chemical balance," he instructed me.

My travels and entertainment had to cease as I received word that Ferencz was back in the Sárvár region. The Turks had threatened the area, and had sacked several nearby villages. Shortly after Darvulia and I returned, we were greeted by a member of Ferencz's garrison, who had been sent ahead to instruct us to stay inside the castle.

Hours later, rocks, arrows and fireballs were sent hurling over the castle's outer fortress walls. My troops stood ready and returned ample fire, forcing the Turks to rethink their strategy. During a lull in the exchange of fire, Ferencz's garrison caught the Turks by surprise and slaughtered them nearby the moat. Bodies of Turkish soldiers floated in the murky waters, staining it red with blood. Stinging serpent eels, brought in by Ferencz to populate the moat a few years earlier, swarmed over the floating bodies.

Although Ferencz was right outside the castle walls, he set up an encampment with his garrison and stood vigil in case the Turks attacked again. I longed for him to come into the castle, but I knew he was where he needed to be.

When Ferencz felt it was safe, he and his troops stationed themselves within Sárvár. He had sustained an injury to his chest, which he begged off as nothing to worry about when Darvulia tried to treat him.

An infection within his wound festered and he became very ill and feverish. With rest, he regained some of his strength, but he never had the same vigor again. He finally retired at Sárvár. He puttered around in the gardens, read books, and involved himself in the printing presses built by his father.

I saw very little of Ferencz, and he did not visit my chambers often. Much of his youthful vigor had escaped him, and although I wanted to be with him and discuss his melancholy, I did not want to insult him or seem pushy by offering uninvited attention. Although I missed him, I kept myself occupied with younger servant boys and young men of the lower gentry.

One of my favorites was a young man named Ádám. He was the son of a local shoemaker, whose father wanted him to take over the family business. Ádám wanted nothing to do with his father's ideas and took to being lazy. I met him when he delivered some shoes I had ordered. We were both thunderstruck by lust. As he placed a shoe on my foot, he massaged my sole with his hands, and then ran light kisses up my leg. He looked at me with his beguiling brown eyes, framed by a full head of curly dark hair. I took him to my bed that instant, and hated the thought of ever letting him leave. He always came back, full of lust and longing. Blissfully, we toiled away the hours that he should have been working.

Darvulia came to me one afternoon, just after

Ádám had left the castle.

"I think one of our laundresses is engaged to Ádám, and is in the stages of planning their wedding," she reported.

"So, what of it? I have no permanent use for the boy."

"Word has been going around that she knows you've been with him and plans to do you harm should you continue your tryst."

"Really? That I should like to see. Bring her to me."

Darvulia returned with the laundress, who had been working on an ornate floral headdress for her wedding, which she clutched in her hands.

"I care not what your name is, or that you work in my household. My interest in bringing you here is to confront you about your threats to my person."

The girl sniveled back a cry and said, "Your Excellency, I have meant no malice toward you, I have been distraught that Ádám has been with you and I—"

"Cease! Do not speak any further. You are speaking out of line." I walked over and slapped her across the face.

"No, please, I beg your forgiveness!"

"You will pay for spreading your rumors of harming me. I hear you are planning a wedding, are you not?" I looked down at the ornate headdress she had made, which she had dropped on the floor.

The girl nodded. She shivered with fear. Darvulia retrieved the headdress and some pins from my dressing table.

"Very well, then. I shall be the first to congratulate you." I pinned the headdress to the girl's head, sinking the pins into her skull. She collapsed at my feet.

Darvulia dragged her off of my feet so that her blood would not damage my new shoes.

"Have Ficko cut off her head and place it on a stake outside of the laundry area. That shall remind the other servants about the woes of spreading rumors."

When I visited the laundry area that evening, I could see the girl's head, mounted high upon a stake, her gauzy veil blowing in the breeze. Ádám never returned.

I sat in my bedroom, enjoying a book and some strong tea one afternoon. Darvulia came running in, interrupting my thoughts.

"My lady, come at once. Your husband is not well." We walked quickly to his chambers, where he lay on his bed, feverish and in pain.

The wound he had received in his last battle with the Turks had festered over the last two years. The injury pained him, but he did little to keep it clean, and he would not let my apothecary or Darvulia treat him. The fetid smell and oozing fluid from the wound made me nauseated.

"Dear husband, why will you not allow us to treat your wound?" I sat alongside of him on his bed.

"It is no matter, I wish to pass from this world soon," he said, sounding tired and defeated. His breathing was labored.

"No my love, it is not your time."

"Yes, my wife. It is close. I am so very sorry for our recent distance, and that I have not been with you by your side. This festering wound has such a stench, I did not wish to expose you to it."

He paused to catch his breath, and then went on, "You have been my greatest joy in life, and I have fought all of my battles for you. You have given me beautiful children, managed our lands with the greatest of ease, and have been a loyal and faithful wife. I commend you, and in the next life, I hope to be with you again."

"I will cross the never ending sea of time to be with you again, my love," I said, as I kissed his lips through tears, which streamed down my face.

I sat by Ferencz's side for many days. I had no interest in food or sleep. I felt an urgent need to be with him, as if my presence could halt his death.

Our children were sent word about their father's condition, and they all traveled to Sárvár from various points. It was January, but all three of them made the trip quickly, despite the cold and snow. Our oldest daughter Anna lived nearby, and had wed Miklós Zrinyi, a Hungarian general and close brother in arms to Ferencz during their battles against the Turks. Katalin returned from Castle Poszóny, where she and her husband were installed to assist Margit, and Paul returned from his studies at Varonnó.

They all arrived just in time for Ferencz's funeral and his interment next to their grandparents, Orsolya and Tamas.

I spent several hours washing Ferencz's body after he died. I gave strict orders that no one interrupt me in my ritual of saying goodbye to my husband. His long, lean body was stretched out flat on the cold marble slab in the castle morgue. I removed his clothes and washed his skin with herbs and fresh water, carefully rinsing the festered wound on his chest. The herbs tempered the rancid smell of the injury. His skin had turned greenish in color around the wound, and spread toward his neck. I took his hand, washed it, and kissed the fingertips, wishing they would come alive with warmth and stroke my cheek the way he always did. I ran the cloth along his face, and I lightly kissed his cold lips, remembering when they had been full of warmth—*oh how I longed for him to return that kiss!*

The cold water made a pleasant sound in the ceramic bowl as I twisted the excess out of my linen wash cloth. Water trickled down his muscular thigh and I ran the cloth up and down his long, well-shaped legs. His penis, that powerful part that could pleasure, impregnate and humiliate, was limp between his legs. I washed it, grateful to have his children and so many years of pleasure with him.

When I finished cleaning Ferencz's body, I wrapped a white linen shroud around him in a motherly fashion. I laughed to myself, *As if I could keep him warm!* I instructed Ficko to handle Ferencz's body with the highest degree of care.

Hundreds of mourners attended Ferencz's funeral, including his troops, nobility of the kingdom, and Ferencz's extended family. I managed to pull together the entire event without much assistance. The castle was full of visitors up until the day after the funeral, and this kept my mind occupied away from my grief.

I was exhausted when it was all over, and I savored my time alone. I found myself visiting Ferencz in the crypt, talking to him and bringing him flowers just as I had for my own sisters in the past.

Fourteen

I sat alone in my chambers, smoking hashish from a Turkish hookah that Ferencz had given me before he died. I savored the heady aroma and distance it took me away from reality.

I missed Ferencz terribly. Things would never be the same without him. I slept in his bed the first few nights after his death. I rolled over to that familiar spot worn into his mattress; he always slept in the center of the bed, even when I shared it with him. I expected comfort from the echoes of his shape, but I found nothing but the coldness of his absence.

A new servant had arrived at Sárvár. She was the woodland priestess Dorotta, Ficko's cousin. She assisted Darvulia and Katalin in tending to my personal needs.

As time wore on, I found Dorotta to be pleasant, and like Darvulia, calming to my nerves. She was obedient, faithful and reliable, and she helped lift my spirits. I spent a great deal of time assembling staff that held those qualities, and I paid them well to stay in service.

The spring of 1604, I moved the household to

Castle Čachtice. Seeing the breathtaking mountains and green meadows helped me lose my skin of grief. I needed the change, and I did not wish to return to Sárvár as there were too many memories of Ferencz. Every direction I turned, there was something that reminded me of him; from the frescoes in the hallways depicting him triumphant in battle, to his chambers filled with his masculine scent. I could hear his soul calling to me from his crypt, begging me to visit him. I could not stand the torment any longer, and I felt relieved when I looked back to see Castle Sárvár shrinking in the distance as my carriage delivered me to Čachtice.

My mood was depressed and temperamental. Punishments were delivered quickly and were severe, even for minor offenses. I had brought my Hanging Cage with me to remind the servants of how severe the punishment could be.

Dorotta made me potions to soothe my melancholy, and she also concocted an improved recipe devised from Péter's skin potion.

"I am almost out of this solution for my skin. Do you think you could make more? I can send for the ingredients from Péter at Sárvár if necessary."

"No, that shouldn't be needed. I can already tell just by its smell what is in it," she said, sure of herself. Her large nostrils flared as she inhaled the aroma of the mixture.

"Its primary element is blood from a virgin. He mixed it with other things to prevent its thickening."

"Hmm, yes, I see. I shall have something ready for you this evening, my lady."

True to her word, she returned with a mixture that was identical to Péter's. Darvulia helped apply the mix to my skin, and then massaged me with olive oil.

Dorotta drew me a warm bath, in which I soaked as they finished rinsing me. My skin felt refreshed, as always.

"I will continue to look for ways to improve upon this mixture, my lady," Dorotta said.

"Wonderful, I will applaud you if you can come up with something that works better." I doubted she could produce better results.

She surprised me a week later with a new potion.

"Try this on a small bit of your skin and see what you think," she instructed.

I moistened the skin of my hand with the dark red ointment. Dorotta covered this area with a white cream, and then rinsed it with water. My skin turned a pale ivory white, and felt smooth and supple.

"This is magnificent! What did you do to improve Péter's ingredients?"

"I used a different kind of blood and a few different herbs. The cream is a mixture of almond oil, mare's milk and lanolin."

"You used a different kind of blood? You mean that of an animal?"

Dorotta smiled, "No my dear, the blue blood of a noble girl." I looked back at her, stunned. She continued, "You have been using the blood of servants, have you not? The blood of a noble is of better quality, for many reasons. They eat well, they are well taken care of, and they do not dally in the sun, which would ruin their skin. Their beauty is extracted and passed along to you, my lady."

"This makes sense, you are right, the blood would be of much higher quality. But at what price? We must be very careful in securing girls for this purpose," I warned her.

"Not to worry, Ficko and I were discreet when we

captured this girl," she said, holding the bottle up to the light. "A steady supply would almost guarantee you the fine skin you desire."

"I will think about this and later instruct you on the procurement of a reliable and safe supply."

I pondered the question of where I would find noble blood on a regular basis. It was risky, but I would have done anything to remain young—anything. I thought of my mother, time rotting her body into a slumped heap of bones and blistered skin before she died. I shivered and dedicated myself to finding a way to avoid old age.

Aside from finding my fountain of eternal youth, I kept up to date with happenings within the Hungarian Empire. When Ferencz was alive, I received regular reports at Sárvár. Since he had died, I had to be tenacious in obtaining the reports, as it was important to me to be apprised of political information.

Protestant and Bohemian rebels had grown tired of Emperor Rudolf's rule, and had started a rebellion against him. The aging emperor's family had forced him to cede his power to his younger brother Matthias to protect the interests of the empire. Matthias had a better relationship with the revolutionaries and was able to reach a truce. They agreed to peace as long as Emperor Rudolf was no longer in power. Matthias was in complete control of the empire's affairs. Rudolf's health had been ailing, and he soon died, leaving Matthias the title of Holy Roman Emperor.

King Matthias took over lands, revenues, and debts that Rudolf had left behind. There was a large debt due to the House of Báthory-Nádasdy for funding the everlasting wars against the Turks, which he neglected to pay. I had sent many notices for the debts to be reconciled, but they went ignored for several years.

The estates I inherited from Ferencz, as well as my own family's estates were bringing in strong revenues. Sárvár sold not only agricultural products, but printed publications from its presses. Ecsed and Varonnó both produced some of the finest wines in Hungary. Čachtice brought in a small income from agriculture, but it did not generate the kind of money I would have liked to have seen. I decided to open up an unused wing of the castle to start a refining school for girls. This would serve my need for revenue as well as the need for noble blood.

Some of the wealthiest families from all over Hungary, Poland and Austria sent their daughters to me to learn etiquette, reading, writing, foreign languages, music, art, mathematics, and science. I hired several tutors, two of which were my own childhood tutors, to serve in the school.

I invited groups of twenty girls per session, and their ages ranged from twelve to twenty. The girls spent their days studying, and their evenings doing chores and learning about castle management, much in the same way Orsolya had taught me in my youth.

The first few groups of girls lived at the castle and graduated within a short time. Word spread that my school was of great benefit to the aristocracy, and I received more applications. I was busy, but it was gratifying work to see the girls arrive with no skills, and graduate with the ability to run an estate.

Dorotta watched the girls with me as they pranced about the castle, and she helped me decide which would be the best specimens for our plans. The first girl we chose was a beautiful Austrian girl named Viktoria. She had wide-set blue eyes, long blonde hair the color of straw, and fine porcelain skin I coveted the moment I laid eyes on her. She had a habit of licking her full red lips, which I found tantalizing.

"I should like a round with her in my chambers before we extract what we need," I told Dorotta.

Dorotta lured Viktoria away from her chores and into my suite. She curtsied immediately when she saw me.

"Arise, Viktoria, come here and let me see you," I requested. She stood before me, her eyes downcast. I could tell she was a bit nervous and I wanted her to be at ease. "How old are you, my dear?"

"I am nineteen, Your Excellency."

"I trust that you are enjoying your stay here?"

"Yes, very much so." She looked up and smiled. "I have learned a great deal, which I look forward to taking with me to benefit my future husband."

"Ah, so you are to be married?"

"An alliance with my family has not yet been made, but my parents are in the process of choosing a suitable husband for me."

"That is wonderful. I am glad this school has been useful to you." I looked at her for several moments before I went on. "There are other things besides etiquette and castle management that you should know before you carry on in life," I told her.

"Yes, life has many lessons, my lady."

"Yes, many indeed. Have you ever been with a man?"

She looked surprised by my question. "No my lady, I have not."

"I should like to show you a few things this evening that will benefit you in the future."

"*Things*, my lady?"

"Yes, things you will need to know to be useful to your husband," I explained. I watched her face turn crimson. "Please disrobe and lay on my bed."

"I'm afraid this is all a bit of a surprise, my lady."

"Yes, for me too. But ever since the moment I looked upon your beauty, I knew I needed to further your experiences."

Nervously, she replied, "I am flattered, Your Excellency, truly I am, but I do not think that I am ready for such lessons—"

"Nonsense! Dorotta, please help Viktoria out of her clothes and onto my bed." Dorotta took Viktoria by the arm and started to strip her clothes from her petite frame. Viktoria struggled, but Dorotta landed a hard slap across the girl's pretty face and that ended her resistance.

Viktoria lay on my bed, shyly looking up at me. I removed my gown and climbed into bed next to her. Dorotta had brought me my ivory phallus from my wardrobe. I ran the phallus up and down the girl's leg and then around her pudendum. Her nipples hardened and I licked them softly at first. As I stroked myself with my fingers I moved the phallus in between her labia. She moistened as I stroked her clitoris, and I sank the phallus deeply inside of her. She shrieked in pain, and the ivory of the phallus turned red with her blood.

Dorotta took the phallus and cleaned Viktoria's blood from her legs. I straddled the girl's face and forced her to pleasure me with her tongue. She whimpered as she licked me, which excited me more and brought me to my climax with ease. I allowed Dorotta a turn with Viktoria and then I decided to end the tryst.

"Dorotta, we need to further our plan as the time is getting later."

"Yes, my lady. Here a robe for you, Viktoria, please follow me," she instructed the terrified girl. We led her to the dungeon which housed the Hanging

Cage. Viktoria did not notice the cage at first, but when Dorotta lowered it, the chains that suspended it clanked and creaked, and Viktoria started to scream. Dorotta knocked her unconscious and placed her inside the cage and then raised it up into the air. I had brought with me from Sárvár a single throne, placed where I could see the torture, but out of the way of any blood drippings.

When Viktoria awoke, she immediately stood up, and Dorotta moved the cage side to side, and around and around, to ensure our victim came into contact with the blades inside the cage.

Viktoria screamed in agony as her beautiful skin was sliced and punctured. Dorotta collected the girl's blood in a pan beneath the cage. I instructed Ficko to dispose of the girl in the cemetery near the woods.

I had Viktoria's blood, her life force, extracted to perpetuate my own beauty. The mere possession of her blood made me giddy with happiness.

When Viktoria's parents arrived from Austria to collect her, none of the servants or teachers knew where she had gone, so they called for me.

"Where is our daughter," her father asked.

"I thought you had come for her last week."

"No, we have not been here to collect her until now. Are you saying she left with someone?"

"Yes, someone she knew. He was in his twenties, tall, blond, curly hair."

"Stefan! She's run away with that worthless piece of refuse!" Her father was angry with the news.

"I am sorry, but he said he was a relative."

"It is all right, it is not your fault, Your Excellency. Thank you for your help. We will find her, and when I get a hold of him..." He walked out with his wife to start their search for Viktoria.

Finding blood for my uses was easier since I had a fresh renewable source within my own castle. On most occasions, Dorotta and Darvulia would assist me in some method of torture before we took blood from our victims. It had become a game of sorts, one that empowered me and brought me much pleasure. I used Dorotta's potion on my skin nearly everyday, and needed at least one girl every week to satisfy the amount of fresh blood required in Dorotta's formula. When we did not have the need for a noble girl, we would sometimes lure a servant girl into the dungeon just to amuse ourselves.

Dorotta had taken to chanting over me as she would paint me with her potions. It was soothing, like the brush that lapped at my skin. I could feel the manifestation of the victim's loveliness and youth soak into my body and soul, renewing my vigor and beauty.

Many of the servants were afraid of Dorotta. There had been rumors of devil worship and midnight séances in the cemetery led by her. Her presence made many people uncomfortable. She was an extremely dark and hairy woman. Her facial features were a bit exaggerated; her aquiline nose was large and ended at flared nostrils. Her eyebrows were knitted together to form one dark line across her forehead. She had wavy dark hair, which she often whipped around over her shoulder, rarely looking to see who she hit with it. She was heavy and large boned, and her posture was poor and often slouched. She rarely trimmed her nails, and she filed them into sharp points and tinted them with dark colors.

I admired Dorotta for her sense of power, her

expertise in alchemy, and her companionship in general. She and Darvulia got along well. Katalin did not speak much to her, but she was never rude and did not seem fearful, even though Dorotta bullied her somewhat. Ficko was deeply in love with Dorotta, although his feelings for her were unrequited. She teased him, offered him sexual favors, and invited him to some of our torture sessions with young girls. More often than not, while I was amusing myself with a girl, Dorotta was off in a corner with Ficko.

Ficko enjoyed joining in our torture sessions. He had a wooden spiked club which he prized as his own handmade tool. He would bludgeon a girl with his club, and in just a few hits, she would be dead. I complained that he killed our victims too quickly, and requested that he not use the club unless I specifically allowed it. Childlike in temperament, he agreed begrudgingly.

Each body was disposed of by Ficko and another trusted servant named Ilona. Ilona was a decrepit old woman with wild gray hair and a wrinkled up face that reminded me of a dried apple. She was hired as a laundress, but she had the brute strength of an ox, and even though she was short and old, she could throw a corpse over her shoulder with great ease. The two would wander out into the cemetery in the middle of the night, hauling shovels and our victims through the dark grassy turf. There were no markers placed over the new graves, but Dorotta would often plant flowers around the graves as she whispered incantations over the newly-tilled earth.

One of the windows from my chambers gave me a grand view of the castle gardens, forest and cemetery. I knew that if I saw a fresh planting of flowers in the cemetery, a burial had been completed successfully.

Fifteen

I received an invitation from King Matthias to attend a banquet in Vienna, to celebrate his kingship, and honor his noble patrons. The invitation was addressed to the Countess Nádasdy, which I found amusing as no one ever referred to me by my husband's surname. The House of Báthory was higher ranking, and Ferencz had added my name to his own because of the status and wealth mine boasted.

I traveled back to Castle Schönbühel where the late Emperor Rudolf had entertained Ferencz and me on our last retreat to Vienna. Seeing the castle brought back many memories, both good and bad, of our stay there years before. I did not like staying at the castle when Rudolf had invited us, and I did not like it any better when Matthias invited me. Both men gave me an uneasy feeling. I felt uncomfortable around Emperor Rudolf because of the way he leered at me, even though there were rumors that he was homosexual and had no interest in women. I was ill at ease with King Matthias because of the fact that he owed me quite a large sum of money. I was surprised Matthias had invited me because I was sure he realized that I would try to collect the debt, or at a minimum, broach the subject if I were given the chance.

Castle Schönbühel was just as ostentatious as it had been during my last visit. King Matthias had redecorated in a more garish manner than had his predecessor. There was cloth of gold and gilded furnishings everywhere one looked. The banquet was just as overdone as the rest of the castle. Tall golden candelabras held slender golden candlesticks, which cast flickering light around the tables. Foods were served on solid gold plates, and sat alongside solid gold utensils. Trenchers, chalices and chargers were all solid gold without one drop of another color to offset the gaucheness.

When I saw the king arrive at the feast hall, I nearly laughed out loud. His clothing matched his furnishings almost identically. His French doublet and slops had been cut from the same brocade fabric as his settee in the foyer. Gold, gold, gold; there was too much gold. I thought to call him King Midas but I withheld my thoughts as he received me.

"Your Majesty." I curtsied as I greeted him.

"Ah, good, Countess Erzsébet, so good that you could attend. I hope you are in good health."

"Yes, thank you for inviting me, and good health to you," I replied, not meaning a word of what I had said. I was happy he did not detain me long. He said the same perfunctory words to the next noble in the receiving line.

King Matthias had me seated at the high table, near his own seat. I took the opportunity to raise the issue of the debts owed to my estate.

"My lady countess, I do hope that you are enjoying the feast."

"Yes, very much so, Your Highness. It has been

a while since I have taken the time to enjoy such an event, since Ferencz's passing."

"I wish to convey to you my deepest sympathies for your loss. It is truly a great loss to all of the empire. He was an impressive fighter and brilliant strategist."

"Yes, he was. I am very proud of his accomplishments. His works have brought much prosperity to the empire. The House of Báthory-Nádasdy has funded a great portion of the military campaigns." I looked at him with interest as I brought up the subject of money.

"Yes, many households have assisted the crown in this endeavor." He seemed nervous at my mention of funding. He fingered his jewel-encrusted chalice as he spoke.

"I am confident the crown will be repaying some of those debts to ensure the future prosperity of the supporting households." I took in a long sip of wine from my plain gold chalice.

"Yes, I will have the treasury look into the matter." With that, he turned to another conversation at the table and ignored me for the remainder of the feast.

The one saving grace of the evening was the entertainment. Matthias had hired a singer to entertain his hundreds of noble guests. After the meal's remains were cleared away, we turned our attention to Hélèna Harzy, a pale pubescent girl with fiery red curls cascading down around her shoulders. She had large doe-like eyes, plump apricot lips, and the voice of a songbird. As she performed church hymns and folk songs, the audience was awestruck. Her soprano voice held everyone in a trance, including me. The eloquence of her voice, coupled with her beautiful looks made me salivate. At the end of her performance, I went to have a word with Hélèna.

"My dear, your voice is captivating."

"Thank you, Your Excellency." She curtsied low.

"You must come to my home Castle Čachtice this winter and perform there for me."

"I would love to entertain you, and I am flattered," she offered. Her beautiful apple-like cheeks turned a light shade of red, so delicious looking, that I wanted to take a bite as she stood before me.

"Wonderful, I shall send for you as soon as I return home from my visit with the king."

We parted ways, but true to my word, I sent for her the minute I arrived back to Čachtice. She arrived as the first winter snow fell upon the hills and valleys. A blizzard blew in soon afterwards, and stopped all passage in and out of Čachtice and the nearby villages.

I made sure Hélèna had a comfortable suite of rooms, decorated in flesh-colored silk fabrics. I wanted her to feel safe and at home while I observed her.

"Sing for me tonight, I have a sumptuous feast planned in honor of your arrival."

"Yes, I would love to, my lady."

"Were your parents planning on visiting?"

"I do not think they will visit during my stay here. Mother does not travel well in the wintertime."

"Yes, that's understandable. I'm glad you made it in time before the blizzards."

"Yes, just in time. I really love my chambers. The rooms are beautiful and more comfortable than any other castle."

"I am glad you like them. Feel free to stay here as long as you like. I will pester you to sing, though," I teased her.

"I would be happy to sing for any occasion as you request, my lady."

She was such an agreeable young girl. I wanted to

keep her like a songbird in a cage for myself forever. She was so exquisitely beautiful that it pained me to look upon her, or to hear her sweet voice. I wanted to consume every bit of her, for her to become a part of me.

Hélèna stayed at Castle Čachtice for several months. During her stay, she did not notice the sexual tension that had built up over time. She was an innocent little virgin, with a naïveté about her that made her even more attractive to me.

I chose the finest minstrels to accompany her pristine voice. She would sing for me at dinner time, before bed, or when I awoke. Everything about her soothed me, and at the same time, tore me apart with desire.

One evening, as Hélèna was singing me to sleep, I asked her to lie next to me. She obliged my request and climbed onto my large four-poster bed. She continued to sing and looked very sleepy. Her voice trailed off as she yawned and fell asleep next to me.

I turned to face her and observed her in the shadows of the night. Her lips fell open slightly as she breathed softly. I leaned over and kissed her, lingering for a moment. She did not awaken, so I went further in my exploration of her body.

She wore an old linen chemise, softened with time and wear. I slipped my hand down the front of it and cupped her budding breast. I traced her pink nipple with my hot tongue and she stirred a little, but did not wake. My hands roamed to her legs, over and between, to that soft wet paradise. My tongue found her clitoris and as I licked her, she moaned. I nibbled a bit and she woke up, startled by my bite.

"My lady! What are you doing?" She looked down at me, my face between her legs. I sunk my teeth into her fragile parts and she let out a howl. I chewed the flesh of her nether region, her legs, and worked my way back up to her breasts. She screamed and tried to fight me off, but I was stronger and held her down. I could not stand looking at her luscious cheeks any longer, and I sank my teeth into the left side of her face. Hélèna screamed and then fainted, and I continued to enjoy her flesh like a wolf would feast on a rabbit.

When Hélèna was conscious, she looked at me in horror. Her face and throat were punctured and bloody, her body was bruised and marked with the imprints of my teeth. I called for Darvulia and Dorotta.

"Bring several buckets of cold water to my terrace doors," I instructed. They returned with four buckets of freezing water. I pushed Hélèna outside into the icy winter night, where she stumbled and fell into the snow.

She cried, and as the winter winds whipped around her, the tears on her face froze.

"Stand up!" I ordered her. She rose to her feet, shaking violently with fear and cold. "My songbird will be forever captured in a crystalline cage," I sang to her in an off-key voice.

Dorotta and Darvulia poured the freezing water over Hélèna's slender body. She shrieked as she was hit with the water, and in shock, she fell to the ground unconscious.

"Stand her up. If you have to prop her up in the snow, do it."

The two women planted Hélèna's legs into the deep snow. She was buried up to her hips. They continued to pour water over her body in various installments. By the middle of the night, Hélèna was completely frozen into a pillar of ice. Instead of sleeping, I sat inside looking out the window, regarding my new statue, as

I sat warm by the roaring fire in the fireplace.

When the morning sun shined its first fingers of light over the surrounding snow-covered mountains, I had Ficko remove Hélèna and bury her in the snow of the forest. The wolves would enjoy her in the spring as much as I did that night.

Gépy and Olyra Harzy arrived at Castle Čachtice the following spring. They had planned to gather their daughter and take her to begin another singing tour to entertain dignitaries all over the Hungarian Empire.

They were not well-dressed, and although they were not paupers, they depended upon their daughter's singing talents for their income.

"Greetings, Your Excellency, we have come to collect our daughter from your care." Gépy humbly bowed his head before me as he spoke.

"Your daughter, Hélèna? She is not here at Čachtice," I told them, mocking a shocked look for their benefit.

"What do you mean? She was supposed to come here to entertain you this past winter, was she not?" Olyra asked, confused.

"She has not been here at this castle. I remember sending word to her, asking her to perform for me, but I would not have asked her to travel in the harsh winter weather. We had one of the worst winters I can recall in this region."

"She took a carriage here. The driver was traveling to Poland after dropping her here. Holy Father in heaven, where is she?" Gépy cried.

"Perhaps the carriage never made it here? I will send out some footmen as soon as the last of the snow melts."

Looking downcast, they agreed to wait a few weeks. I instructed Ficko to lead a search for the girl's body.

Off into the woods the search party went, to scour the countryside for Hélèna. They returned with a litter carrying remnants of her body, torn into shreds by wolves.

Gépy and Olyra were beside themselves with anguish. I allowed them to bury what was left of their daughter in the cemetery. I could not wait for them to leave as their grief depressed me.

I sent Gépy and Olyra to Castle Poszóny for a brief stay on their way back to Vienna, along with a satchel of money, which seemed to heal their grief as soon as they saw how much was in the bag.

My finishing school was bringing in more applications than I could accept each year. I was pleased with the tutors and the success rate of the graduates.

Aside from the business accomplishments of the school, I was pleased to have an assortment of beautiful girls around me at all times. Some were very willing to entertain my carnal urges, but they were not as exciting as the ones who were unwilling. Ficko had devised a number of torture devices, set up in an organized fashion in the castle dungeon. He had installed a special drainage system to drain all of the fouled blood from the floors into the moat. This saved Ilona and Dorotta much time in cleaning up the mess after a torture.

Darvulia had taken ill, much to my dismay. Dorotta and Katalin had twice the amount of work to do as Darvulia became bedridden. Her limbs and joints were sore and she could barely walk to the privy. She developed small white sores around her mouth and tongue, which prevented her from eating or drinking. An angry red rash covered her skin, and just the feeling of a sheet touching her body sent her over the edge in pain. Her sight had begun to dim, and she grew disoriented.

I sent for the apothecaries, afraid they would not make it in time to help Darvulia. A group of Zoran's understudies arrived and examined her body.

"Your Excellency, may I have a word with you?" said the youngest of the understudies.

"Yes, what is happening to Darvulia?" I pulled him outside of her room to speak.

"She has what is known as the French disease, *syphilis* is the medical term."

"French disease?"

"Yes, that is what it is often called as the French have it prolifically. It is caused by promiscuity." The young medic blushed as he explained the circumstances of the disease.

"Is there anything you can do to heal her—to make her more comfortable?"

"We can try applications of mercury which may rid her body of the disease, but usually when someone is in this stage, they are beyond our help. I will prepare a poultice for her sores which might make her more comfortable."

I was speechless. Darvulia's death sentence had just been read, and it would be a long-suffering, painful death. I nodded to the application of the poultice, and my mind spun with disbelief that my servant, my friend and trusted confidant was dying. Darvulia was my shadow. Wherever I was, she followed, in total obedience. She tenderly took care of me when I had fits of my falling disease, and she assisted Dorotta with my beauty regimen. She listened to me as I lamented about some unimportant occurrence, all the while, never complaining once.

I looked at Darvulia as she lay in her bed, drowsy, but left behind by the gods of sleep because of her ailment. She was feverish, and her brow was pasty with cold sweat. The apothecaries warned me about contact with her skin.

"Do not touch her sores as this disease is extremely contagious. If she dies, I would recommend burning everything."

"She won't die! You said *if* she dies! She cannot die!" I was distraught. Dorotta and Katalin comforted me as we watched Darvulia slip away.

I was in mourning for several weeks after Darvulia's passing. I had Ficko place her in the cemetery. Dorotta planted a small tree over her grave. My sorrow for her death rivaled that which I had felt for Ferencz when he died.

A few weeks into my mourning, I received word from my oldest daughter Anna that she had lost her first born in childbirth. She wrote me to tell me of her great disappointment and said that her husband Miklós Zrinyi was very angry over the death of their child.

> *He blames me, Mother, I just know he does. He doesn't say he holds me responsible for our son's death, but I can see it in his eyes. He won't allow me to come see you, for he thinks you are a witch. I mean no disrespect, dear mother, but I thought you should know why I am unable to visit you.*

I held the letter close to my heart and cried. Mourning for Darvulia. Mourning for my grandson. Mourning for my daughter's thoughts about me. Nothing consoled me.

My grief rolled itself into rage, and as I tore down the castle halls, I grabbed the hair of a servant girl and dragged her down to the dungeon. I punched her face until she was unconscious, and then lowered the Hanging Cage, readying it for the girl's entry.

After I placed the girl inside of the cage, I raised it in the air and waited for her to regain consciousness. I sat in my throne for over an hour and the girl never woke. My anger flared higher because I did not even have the pleasure of torturing someone. I left the dead girl in the cage and I ran through the castle, flinging small pieces of furniture, paintings, and whatever else I could get my hands upon, through the air at servants and guards.

My heart raced in my chest. I felt like I could not get back in control of myself. Dorotta found me, cowering in a corner of an unused room. She held me tightly and absorbed my tears into her soul.

"I know that I will never be able to replace Darvulia, but please, let me step in and take care of you, my lady." I nodded into her heavy and comforting bosom, drained of tears.

Sixteen

took a carriage ride into the village marketplace as I usually did each year to survey and meet with the local business owners. I purchased some books, candles, and some beautiful embroidered foreparts. On the way back to the castle, I stared out my window, watching as the scenery rambled by. The mountainside was in full bloom, filling the air with the heavy perfume of nature. Trees were crowned and mantled in fluttering leaves. They produced the softest of natural music in harmony with the songbirds, perched within their branches.

The motion of the carriage and the lulling sounds of the forest were pulling me into sleep. Before my eyes shut, I caught a glimpse of a dark wolf—or what I thought was a wolf. I rubbed my eyes and took another look. It was a man, tall, dark and lean, staring at me from the outskirts of the forest. He was sinewy, and moved like a predator on the hunt. His long dark hair fell around his shoulders, and was capped with a black scarf. He was dressed in black breeches, shiny spurred black boots, and a billowy black shirt. He stood beside a tree and watched as my carriage drove down the path toward Castle Čachtice. Our gazes were locked momentarily, but when the carriage hit a bump, my line of sight was interrupted. When I returned my gaze to where I thought the man stood, he had vanished.

A few days later, I saw the wolf-man again, out near the edge of the forest. I got up from my seat and went out into the cemetery.

"You there, come here so that I may see you," I called to the man. He walked forward, his gaze never leaving my own. "What is your name and from where do you come?"

"I am László and I am a wanderer." He did not bow or show the respect due to my station.

"Do you realize who I am?"

"I gather that you are a noble. It is of no importance to me."

"It should be."

"Ranks, titles, lands given and taken away. It is all a game of politics that I care not to involve myself with." His brilliant green eyes were wide-set and looked to be lined with kohl.

"What then, do you involve yourself with?"

"As I said, I am a wanderer. I live off of the land."

"A thief?"

"Never. I have no need to steal from others. I hunt for my food."

I found him to be enigmatic. He was fine-looking, yet coarse. A stranger, yet familiar to me. As I watched him move I felt a yearning to learn more about him.

"Come in and dine with me, I should like to know more about you."

He shook his head. "There is no more to learn about me, lady friend, and I have already had my meal for the evening."

"Then sit with me while I eat, I am starving for both a meal and good company. I wish to know about your travels, what compels you to live the way that you do. Come in." I held my hand out to him. He paused to think for a moment and then accepted my hand.

As I ate my roasted lamb, I fired questions at László from all directions. He would not have had the chance to eat if he'd had a plate in front of him.

"You were a noble before this nomadic life, were you not?"

"How did you know?"

"I can tell a blue blood from a pauper. Why on earth would you choose this life over a life of opulence?" I asked, stuffing food into my mouth.

"I had no choice. I lost my lands to the Turks and the king would not assist me in fighting back. My household burned to the ground, my entire family died. My wife raped and burned, my children tortured and killed, all in front of me."

"I am so sorry that you have known this grief. My late husband was vehement in his fight against those bastards while he lived." I placed my hand over his in comfort.

"It happened years ago, though I am still scarred from the experience, but I push on. After I let go of everything, life became simpler, easier to take." He caressed my hand in return.

"Are you sure you would not like a plate of supper?"

"No, but I thank you for your kindness, my lady. What is your name?"

"I am Countess Erzsébet Báthory."

"My apologies for my lack of respect, dear lady. And you are widowed as well?"

"Yes, Ferencz died a few years ago. Worry not about

my station. I felt more at ease before you knew about it."

"It seemed as though it was important to you when I first approached your home."

"I have found that in talking with you, the politics of my station sets me apart from many people who interest me. It is easier to learn more about you when we are on the same level, wouldn't you agree?" He nodded. I went on, "Join me for a walk in the gardens."

We walked, arm in arm, throughout the gardens and orchards. We talked for hours about family, growing up, politics, and our former spouses. I felt like I had known him forever.

"You seem very familiar to me," he turned and said as we sat beneath the shade of a tree, watching the sun set on the horizon.

"You feel that way to me as well." I looked over at him. He leaned over and kissed me, softly at first, and then more urgently.

We kissed all the way back to my chambers. I called to Dorotta and instructed her that there would be no interruptions of my privacy, and then I secured the doors.

László and I were locked in a fiery embrace, kissing, feeling, caressing. Our lovemaking was passionate, but he did not stir the same excitement within me as Ferencz had done. László was gentle, whereas Ferencz was savage.

We slept afterwards, and when I awoke early the next morning, I found that László had slipped away. On the bedside table, there was a small bouquet of wildflowers and a note that read, *"Thank you, Your Wanderer."* László did not wander back into my woods again.

Dorotta had brought me many beautiful girls for my entertainment. Some were slender and some were plump; there were hair, skin and eye colors of all shades. They all seemed to blend together after a while. I kept short notes about each girl, what I liked and what I did not. It gave them all humanity, because as I was torturing each of them, they were surreal to me. I wanted their beauty, their youth, their innocence, and I tried tearing it from them using whatever device amused me.

One evening, we were occupied torturing a young student named Kristina from Győr. She was a buxom girl of nineteen, with long brown hair and a cherubic face with dimpled cheeks—the type of cheeks I fancied biting as they reminded me of apples. Dorotta dragged the girl by the hair down the hallway to the dungeon. She tied her up on top of a table, legs apart. After using needles to prod her skin, I oiled some paper and rolled it up and shoved it between her legs. Dorotta lit the paper on fire and we watched as the girl screamed, unable to free herself. We allowed her pubic hair to be scorched, and then doused her with icy cold water. She fainted, and I called for Ficko to place her in the Hanging Cage.

I was distressed when I had to leave my entertainment because one of the servants came down to retrieve me.

"Your Excellency, I am sorry to disturb you, but the Palatine Thurzó is here to see you."

"Here at this hour? Very well, I shall receive him in the council room. Ficko, do what you will with the girl."

I went to my chambers and changed my clothing.

After checking my hair and jewelry, I proceeded to meet the palatine. Count György Thurzó was a distant cousin of mine, whom I had not seen since my wedding. I regarded him before I entered the room. He had a thick, scraggly beard, which I found repulsive. His nose was curved like a bird's beak, and his ears were a bit too small for his head. I straightened my spine and walked into the meeting room.

"Palatine, what a pleasure it is to see you, even at this hour."

"Good evening, dear cousin. It is also a pleasure to see you. I apologize for the hour, but I just arrived in from the eastern principalities, where I had some business to attend to for the king."

"What can I do for you, sir?"

"The king wanted me to stop and visit with you and discuss the recent sales of some Nádasdy properties."

"I sold both Báthory and Nádasdy lands. Bécko, Keresztúr... it was all done to relieve some of the strain placed upon my household by the crown's unpaid debts."

"I see, well it did catch the attention of the king."

"I do hope that he plans to repay the large debt he owes me."

"In good time, I am sure. I see your etiquette school has had quite the positive influence on many of its graduates."

"Yes, it has been a huge success. I may expand it in the future."

"There has been some talk about girls who were expected to attend not coming home. Have you heard of any runaways?"

"Yes, I believe there were a few girls who never made it to the castle, but none ever ran away after arriving."

"I venture to guess that they fell in love and eloped against their parent's wishes. That is often the story."

"Yes, girls that age do become love-struck easily."

"Well, I won't take up anymore of your time, dear cousin. I must be going."

"Would you like to stay here at Čachtice for the evening? You've traveled an awfully long way."

"No, but I do thank you for your offer of hospitality. I am due at the constable's house this evening. I shall return in a few weeks for a longer visit."

"Please do. I will show you out."

After the palatine left, I felt my heart race inside my chest. It was one thing for servant girls to be discovered dead, but the rumor of missing noble girls would raise quite a stir. I called Dorotta, Ficko and Ilona into my chambers.

"We will need to be certain that if anymore noble girls are slain, to be careful of where they are buried. I just had a brief visit from the palatine, and I am sure he will be back."

"Yes, my lady. I am very careful with the bodies. Do you wish there to be a new method of disposal?" Ficko asked.

"No, I think the current burial practice is acceptable, but we must be very sure not to be seen as the girls are buried. Is this understood?" They all nodded and then I dismissed them.

The next day, my daughter Anna visited the castle unexpectedly.

"Anna, it is good to see you, but I was not expecting you. Are you traveling alone?"

"Greetings, Mother. Yes, I know it is unexpected, and I did travel alone here to talk to you about something important. Is there somewhere we can speak privately?"

"Yes, this way to my council room." I led her to the room and shut the door.

"Mother, I overheard my husband speaking to the palatine a few days ago about you."

"Really? I just had a visit from the palatine last night."

"Thurzó told Miklós that he was planning on going forward with an investigation."

"An investigation? For what purpose?"

"From what I understood, the king does not wish to repay his debts to you, and is looking for a way out to nullify the debt. If he can arrest and convict you for some wrong doing, then he will be free of the debt and will seize your remaining assets."

I sat in shock. *So this is why they paid attention when I sold my two properties.*

"Mother, I am worried about you. I think Miklós may be involved in this somehow."

"I never liked your husband. It was a bad idea to join you to him. He always struck me as dishonest."

"I am sorry Mother, he has not spoken of any of this to me directly. As I said, I overheard them talking. They were in the middle of fabricating rumors."

"Rumors? Of what sort?"

"They said that they would spread the word that you were murdering noblewomen, and practicing witchcraft. There were other things, but those two were the worst offenses."

"So they seek to stain my reputation? Good luck to them. They'll need it." I felt my stubborn streak rise to the occasion. Let them do what they will. No one would believe them.

"I hope that you will be safe, Mother. I am worried about you." Anna embraced me and I kissed her forehead. She was a lovely auburn-haired girl, with the chiseled features of her father. I looked into her eyes and saw him staring back at me.

"I will be fine, my dear. Not to worry. I have weathered many storms throughout life. Now, how long will you be staying with me?"

"My visit will need to be short as I must return to Miklós."

Anna visited with me for a few days and then left, leaving me feeling worried about my future. I was fortunate to have her forewarning about events to come.

Several months after Anna's visit, Palatine Thurzó returned, unannounced, this time with armed guards.

"Countess, I must have a word with you," he said in a stern voice.

"What, pray tell, is the problem?"

"I am ordered by His Majesty King Matthias to initiate an investigation into the disappearances of two noble girls, who were accepted into your school of manners."

"I do not know of what you are talking about, but I have no reason to be uncooperative. Feel free to search around all you like."

"Thank you for your cooperation, Countess." He bowed his head slightly, and then called his officers to prepare for the search of Castle Čachtice.

The most evidence the search party found was some blood and soiled garments in the dungeon.

"My lady Countess, I will have to place you under house arrest, as you are a suspect in this investigation. I must insist that you stay in your castle, and do not leave the area for any reason. I shall appoint a few of my garrison to stand by while I complete my case."

"I am under arrest? But I have not done anything!"

"These are orders with backing from the king. Please abide by them."

"This is all about the king's debt to me, isn't it? I know what you're doing and I will fight you every step of the way!" I flew out of the room and into my chambers.

Thurzó had confiscated the soiled clothing and a few instruments of torture. He had also found one of my journals, the one that listed my torture victims and their various traits, although in it, I did not allude to any of the girls being of noble birth.

He was happy with what he had found, because he thought it would help build a case against me. I knew better. As Countess, I was untouchable. None of what they could prove led to the deaths of any noble girls. At best, they could prove I tortured my servants, but what noble did not? Thurzó had a long fight ahead of him, as I planned to rail against authority.

A letter from the king arrived with an officer a few days after Thurzó had left. It listed crimes of which I was accused. I was shocked as it listed every girl's name from my torture diary as a victim in Thurzó's case against me. He also accused me of witchcraft and kidnapping. He included a long list of accomplices and witnesses. After I had read the letter, the delivering officer forced me into my chambers and locked me in. I was imprisoned within my own chambers!

For hours, I banged on the doors, and I called for Dorotta and Katalin, or anyone that could hear me, but my calls went unanswered. No one came to my rescue. When a plate of food arrived, delivered by an unknown servant, I realized that my personal staff had been detained as well.

"Where are my servants, Dorotta and Katalin?" I questioned the serving girl.

"I know not, my lady. The palatine took several people from the castle with him back to the king's court." The girl curtsied and left, locking the doors behind her.

My terrace doors would open, but there were guards stationed all around the courtyard. I went out to look around for a few minutes, but one of the guards guided me back in, shut the doors, and then stood nearby. I shut the heavy drapes, and when I looked out again in the morning, the doors had been bricked in. I ran to the hallway doors, but I was shocked to find that they opened to a wall made from heavy bricks. The wall had a small slot at the bottom for the delivery of food.

I sat on my bed, with the realization setting in that I was indefinitely trapped in my suite of rooms. I sobbed and wailed for hours, but it did no good. I was imprisoned.

Seventeen

had no idea what date it was, or how long I had been incarcerated. The passage of time was dreamlike, dates overlapping. I knew that when György Thurzó had first darkened my door with his news of the investigation, it was March of 1610. I had been in my chambers since December of that year. I guessed that I had been detained for at least six months.

My son-in-law Count György Drugét de Homonna, and my son Paul both visited me while I was locked away. They spoke to me through the food slot.

"Dear mother, it is Paul and György, we are here to visit you," my son Paul said. I sat by the door, happy to be able to talk to the two men.

"Paul! My dear son, and György, how is Katalin?" I was so excited I could barely contain myself.

"We are all fine, Mother. It is you we are concerned about. How is your health?"

"I am well, but I am extremely depressed. I want to be released. Has there been any word from the palatine?"

"No, I am afraid there hasn't been. He is scouring the details of this case, and has questioned hundreds of people," György replied.

"I am locked up here like an animal, why won't they let me out to defend myself?"

"They are worried that you will flee from Hungary."

"It would be good for them if I did runaway. The king is so worried about the money he owes me. It would be taken care of if he would just allow me to be free."

"I know Mother, it is a conspiracy, one that both of us are fighting on your behalf," Paul said.

"You will be happy to know that you are a grandmother," György said with enthusiasm.

"Katalin had the baby? Is she well? How are they?"

"Both Katalin and Maria are doing well. Katalin had no problems with the birth, although we all wished you could have been there."

"I wish I had been. I wish I could hold my granddaughter. Paul, what has been happening with you?"

"I have finished my schooling and will be wed to Judith Revay soon."

"Yes, I am sure she will make you a good wife. She is now the Baroness of Treboszto, is she not?"

"Yes, she recently inherited many lands. We are to be wed next summer. I think we will be most happy together."

"Then it was a good arrangement. This is more than I can say for Anna's husband. I believe he was behind this conspiracy with the palatine."

"I wondered what he had to do with the investigation. He seemed to be helping the palatine quite a bit, especially when it came to digging up evidence," Paul said.

"Helping him? He's the one conjuring up most of it, I'll wager. If I ever get out of here, he will be the first person I horsewhip."

"We will do our best to get you out Mother. I have been to court on your behalf, and will continue to pressure the powers that be. Father would be appalled at all of what has happened. We won't allow harm to come to you."

"Thank you, dear sons. I am so glad I have you on my side."

"The guards have prompted us that it is time to take our leave," György said through the slot.

"Be well, Mother, I love you," Paul said. I wished I could embrace him through the door, but I would have to be satisfied with the touch of his fingertips through the food slot.

"I love you, too, both of you. Give my love to Katalin."

"I will. Be well."

After my sons left, I cried mournfully into my bed pillows.

Life was transpiring for everyone else, but not for me. My life stood at an impasse, my freedom was left to the whim of a capricious ruler. I wrote many letters to Palatine Thurzó, and to King Matthias. Thurzó made sure I had copies of all the papers filed by him at the king's court.

Greetings Erzsébet,

> *May this letter find you in good health. Please be patient while the details of our investigation are sorted out carefully. It pains me to tell you that we have found several bodies of young women buried on*

the grounds of your Castle Čachtice. There were also body parts of young girls nearby within the forest.

We do have your diary of names, all of which will be thoroughly investigated accordingly. We have also arrested your personal staff as accomplices in these deeds. They will be scrupulously questioned and will answer for any crimes of their own.

Punishments for these types of crimes, as you may know, are harsh. It has been recommended that you are beheaded at the court of King Matthias. I have advised against this measure to protect the good family name of Nádasdy. We have also kept most of the proceedings private, so as not to bring attention to your predicament.

You are in my prayers,
Palatine György Thurzó

I was astonished. They had all but wrapped up the case against me, without as much as a word from me. I wondered what would become of me. I wrote a reply to Thurzó:

Palatine,

I am the humble servant of the king. It was in error that I requested debts to be repaid to my late husband's estate. If this is what has angered the king, please convey to him that we can forget about such debts.

I am a devout follower of the Lutheran faith, and do not practice witchcraft or anything remotely relating to Satan. There have been no kidnappings or murders. And at worst, I can be accused of nothing more than punishing disobedient servants who required correction.

I believe your evidence has been planted, and your facts are inaccurate.

I beseech you; please allow me to be set free, or at the very least, allow me to come to court to defend myself against these heinous accusations.

Countess Erzsébet Báthory Nádasdy

My words fell upon deaf ears. There was no reply to my correspondence. Neither my son nor son-in-law were successful in speaking in my defense.

It wasn't long before I received a visit from the palatine. He wanted to let me know in person that my servants had been executed. Dorotta and Ilona received the worst of the treatment.

"They were condemned as murderous witches, and their fingers were chopped from their hands. They were set afire and burned at the stake, their souls set free," he said, triumphantly.

"You murderous bastard!" I raged at him through the food slot. He was unaffected by my words.

"Your vile hunchback Ficko was castrated,

beheaded, and his body was burned."

"Stop, no more!"

But he continued on to tell me about Katalin, my longtime servant from Orsolya's regime.

"She could not be proven guilty of any specific crimes, although she was still considered an accomplice to the rest of your staff. She was given a sedative and then burned at the stake alongside the others." The palatine seemed to take great pleasure in knowing my closest servants and confidants were dead.

"They did not deserve this treatment."

"Yes, my dear cousin, your accomplices in crime are dead. I tortured them long and hard to get the evidence I need to put you away for the rest of your pathetic life," he said arrogantly through the food slot.

"You are a malicious and evil man. For whatever reason, you take pride in what you have done. I am innocent of these crimes, yet many people have had to pay with their lives, because you tortured them into saying what you wanted them to say."

"I have done what needs to be done in accordance with His Majesty's wishes. Just be appreciative that you are not to meet your end as your accomplices did, dear cousin. I have done you a favor by seeing that you are kept safely confined behind these walls."

"Burn in hell you, vile beast."

"Ah, more witchcraft. I shall record that this day you put a hex upon my soul."

"Be happy that I never did more to you."

"Good day to you, my lady witch."

I stayed in bed most days, and wished time could be reversed. I wished I could be brought back to my first night with Ferencz, or even as far back as childhood at Castle Ecsed. The loneliness and solitude of my confinement was almost more than I could bear. I found myself talking to servants through the food slot about trivial things, such as the weather.

My meals were spare and bland, and served only once per day in the evening. Typically, I would receive a bowl of broth, some bread, wine, and a small piece of meat. If the cook was feeling generous, I would receive some vegetables or fruit. Prior to my incarceration, I was never a glutton, but I always ate in the morning, which I had missed. I learned to save my bread and fruit for my morning meal. My gowns felt loose, and I knew I had lost weight due to my restricted diet.

My food was always served in the wooden dishes of the servants. I pictured the palatine eating from my fine gold-gilded dishes, throwing his remains onto the tray that was to be mine. I wondered how my estates were being operated in my absence.

The walls of my rooms felt like they were closing in on me. I remembered when I had first seen them; I thought my rooms to be expansive. Imprisoned within them, they were suffocating and small. I started writing random thoughts on the walls, varying from slurs about the palatine and the king, to love poems about Ferencz.

I ceased my skin treatments after I ran out of Dorotta's skin cream. I knew age would set in, and as soon as I stopped the skin treatments, and my skin felt dry as the desert. I rarely changed and could not bathe during my confinement. I had one mirror left, the present Darvulia had given me years before. It was still in perfect condition. Since I had no servants to color my hair, I noticed fine streaks of gray running through it. I brushed it some, but then stopped. I could think of no reason to keep up my hygiene.

I laughed as I looked at the curtains that covered the old terrace window. I would go up to them and throw them open, pretending to be awed by a sunset or sunrise over the Carpathian Mountains. I held court with a legion of dolls from my childhood that had been stored away in my wardrobe. I pretended to be a queen, locked away at the top of a tower.

My mirror began to lie to me about my appearance. Each time I looked into it, I saw a different person staring back. I would look in the mirror and smile, and all of a sudden, my teeth would be missing or broken, or my hair would be unruly at one glance and then beautiful the next.

I read the books that had been left in my chambers over and over several times. There was a Lutheran Bible, which I knew by heart, as well as some books on alchemy, astrology, several mythology compendiums and a handwritten book filled with wisdom by an Asian mystic called *Buddha*. I became mesmerized by a book about Arthurian England, and wondered what it would have been like to have lived in those times.

Aside from theatrics and reading, I had many hours to dedicate to self-examination. It was hard to face my own reflection, not in the tangible sense, but in the spiritual sense.

"All that we are is a result of what we have thought." What a profound statement by the Asian wise man. If this were true, then I was a result of my sadistic thoughts and licentious tastes. I was a result of all of the tortures and beatings I had bestowed upon my servants and noble girls. I was a result of an upbringing by cruel and distant parents. The end result was what I had to face each day in confinement.

I paced the floors, from one room to the next, like a

caged lioness, for that was what I was. Often, I looked around my rooms in search of the least painful way to kill myself. There were satin drapery sashes by which I could hang myself. I could drive the fireplace poker into my heart. I could asphyxiate on my food. There were so many ways to die, but I was too scared to follow through with any of them. For one thing, I never wanted to die, and for another, it would have been ironic if someone came to set me free.

I found the recipe for the scrying potion in Darvulia's Book of Shadows, which I inherited at her death. After digging around in the wardrobe, I found Darvulia's case of dried herbs—not enough to commit suicide as Darvulia always warned me about, but enough to escape one time, if only in my mind, elsewhere.

The recipe was a simple mixture, and still smelled as I remembered it the night I projected into Ferencz's encampment many years before. If only I could go there and be with him again. If I requested that the gods take me to Ferencz, I wondered, would he be in heaven? In hell? Caught within the River Styx or some other purgatory?

I made myself comfortable on my bed. After a while, I let my mind wander, and took the potion with no set destination in mind.

The potion allowed me the freedom that I craved. I could see my soul leave my body resting on the bed. I took the form of a zephyr and soared over the castle rooftops and around towering trees. I saw the guards that milled around the castle gates, the golden color of the wheat fields, and the emerald green color of a nearby lake. I was free, and like the wind, I breezed away from Čachtice. I flew through a steeply carved canyon, and around the peaks of the High Tatras. There was no limit to the heights I could achieve, and

I kept going, untethered by reality.

I kept flying until I saw a beautiful meadow, which was covered in a rainbow of colorful flowers. I landed and inhaled their sweet scents. I gathered several bouquets of flowers, and enjoyed the breathtaking scenery.

When I looked up, I saw a tall, dark haired man approaching me. It was Ferencz. I dropped my flowers. He smiled widely at me and started to run. I ran toward him and we landed in a tight embrace. He looked to be in his thirties again; cleanly shaven, his glorious body was plainly clothed, with no evidence of his chest wound.

"My love, you have come! I have waited so long for you." He caressed my back as he held me, my cheek to his chest.

"I do not ever want to release you again. It was so hard to let you go when you died," I said. Tears filled my eyes.

"I know, I was there watching as you washed me and interred my body. I could feel how heavy your heart was. I longed to come back, but could not."

"Do you know what they are doing to me now?"

He nodded. "Yes, it is a travesty what Matthias is doing. It is a conspiracy, and it is all about greed. He is shrewd and that is how he came about his power, stealing it from Emperor Rudolf. He wants our lands and will take whatever he can get his greedy hands upon, and will never repay the debt he owes."

I gazed at Ferencz, taking in every feature and every line. I inhaled his masculine scent, the one I tried to escape when I left Sárvár.

"Isn't Paul wonderful?"

"Yes, he is a loyal son, and he is doing everything within his power to free you. Unfortunately, it is all for naught. They will not listen to him."

"What should I do? Will I die, confined like an animal to my chambers?"

"No, my love, you will be set free. It may take some time, but you will be free to go wherever you choose."

"Where should I go, dear husband? I wish with all my heart that I could be with you."

"That time will come, dear love, but you are not yet ready for that passage. Go west to Italy and do not look back to our old life. Start anew." He paused and stared into my eyes. "I shall love you for all time, dear wife."

Ferencz started to fade, and I reached out to embrace him one last time. Tears streamed down my face as he kissed my forehead and caressed my cheek. I felt the warmth of his kiss when I awoke in my bed, my arms wrapped around my pillow.

Eighteen

I had been locked away for more than two years when, one morning, I was plagued with another fit of my falling sickness. I fell to the floor with uncontrollable shaking. My entire body seized and stiffened as I lay helpless on the floor. With no one to care for me, I had to tend to myself when I regained direction over my senses. I had lost control of my bowels and defecated in my gown. I had other gowns in my wardrobe, but I always had my servants to assist me in cleaning up after a spell such as this.

Without a bath or a supply of fresh water, I had to wait for the servant to bring the daily dish of food that evening before I could request fresh water. My backside and legs were covered in filth. I had a hard time understanding how a body could produce something so vile. I vomited from the odor and tore my gown from my body. I wiped myself with my silk chemise, which was already soiled from months of sweat. I threw on another chemise, knowing that it would be soiled by the remaining filth that was left on my body.

"Please bring me a bowl of fresh water," I called

through the food slot several times until I heard footsteps approaching my door.

"I am here with your food, my lady. I am not allowed to return again this night," she said.

"But please, I have had an episode of my falling sickness and I need to clean myself. I am filthy. Please bring me some water."

"I shall see what I can do."

The servant left, but did not return that night. I slept on the floor next to the door in my soiled chemise, hoping someone would bring me some water. I felt like a child, unable to clean myself effectively. I hated the disgrace of asking for water and having to tell the lowly servant what it was for, but I had no choice.

The next morning, the servant returned with a shallow bowl of water. I cleaned myself as best as I could manage with a linen cloth. I placed the cloth and my soiled clothes within a sheet. With nowhere else to put the mess, I stuffed it through the food slot. I had most of it pushed through when it became stuck in the slot. *Brilliant,* I thought to myself.

When the servant returned later in the day with my evening meal, she was astonished.

"What do you expect now, my lady? I am not your laundress," she snarled.

"I did not want the soiled gown in the room with me. The smell of it was stifling! What else would you have me do with it?" I yelled back at her through the wall.

"Well, now you've gone and blocked your food slot and the stench is on this side of the door as well as on your side. You've made quite a mess. The palatine will not be happy about this."

She left and returned later with some guards. They were able to dislodge the soiled clothing, after much effort. I heard the guards curse as the soiled items tumbled out onto their feet.

"Take care that you do not do this again, my lady. We are not responsible for your filth. If this should happen again, the palatine shall be notified and there will be consequences," the guard warned me. He told the servant to dispose of the mess and to forgo serving my dinner that night.

I collapsed on my bed. My head ached as it normally did after a fit, and I was terribly thirsty. Darvulia and Dorotta had always made elixirs for me to drink after a fit, which made me feel much better. I missed both of them dearly. Not having them made me realize how much I took them for granted while they were with me. I had taken a great deal for granted over the years.

I thought about my children being away for so long. I hardly knew any of them, yet they were loyal to me. It was better that they had all been sent away from me during their childhood, as they were protected from my lifestyle. I was worried that they would be swayed by the palatine. *What if my personal staff had told them everything before they died? What would my children think of me?* I was better off in my chambers, a savage animal caged.

I slept fitfully, tossing and turning as I tried to escape the dreams that plagued my psyche. They were clear and realistic, and this bothered me. In the first dream, I was back at Castle Ecsed as a child, seated on my mother's lap in an old wooden chair. I wore a white chemise, soft and pristine, edged with Venetian lace.

Mother rocked me and I leaned into her chest, comfortable. The chair squeaked as she moved. I could smell her lavender scented perfume, and I felt the warmth of her body against my own. She rocked, slowly at first, and then started to rock faster and faster; she would not stop or slow down at my protests. When I looked up, her face was pocked with rotted oozing sores, more morbidly than I had seen her before she died. She smiled at me as she rocked; her teeth were blackened and pointed. I clawed to get away from her, but her grasp tightened and she sunk her sharp teeth into my neck. Blood stained my beautiful chemise and I fell from her lap.

When I looked up from the spot where I landed, I was alone in a room back at Castle Sárvár. Ferencz's velvet cloak lay draped across a bench, my paperwork spread across a desk. I remembered my daily routine of business, looking at each estate's revenues, expenses and inventories. The letters on the pages of the account books seemed to crawl around as if they were fluid. I watched the unreadable text swirl together on the parchment. I took Ferencz's cloak and brought it to my nose, inhaling his masculine scent. My heart ached for him. I wanted to go back in time, back to when I could hold him, touch him, and taste him. All I tasted at that moment was salty tears. I rested my head on the desk, and when I looked up, I was in another place.

I was in a garden of an estate I did not recognize. I heard a lady laughing, and searched around the hedges to find her. I tried to follow the sound of her melodic laugh, but I could not see her. I heard grunting and moaning, and when I looked around the labyrinth of shrubs, I saw a woman with long dark hair, naked, straddling a man's lap—the man was Ficko. His head looked to have been sewn on, sutures visible at his neck. He did not appear to see me, and concentrated heartily on his carnal pleasure. When the woman turned her head in my direction I saw her face, and I recognized her as Dorotta. She had no eyes, and her face had been burned. It looked as if the skin had been melted. She did not acknowledge me, and turned back to Ficko.

I walked back through the garden, losing myself within the maze of shrubbery. I turned right, then left, and backtracked. I was disoriented and frightened. As I made my way through the labyrinth, the maze walls turned into people. They were all lined up, side by side, glaring at me as I passed by. As I observed their faces, I recognized them as my victims. Jeselle. Minika. Hélèna. Andrei and his musicians. All the noble girls and servants that I had tortured, assaulted, and murdered over the years. They were all nude so that I could see their scars and punctured skin. The stood at attention like a row of soldiers waiting for battle. One by one they reached for me as I passed. I ran from the maze, screaming, finally finding its end. I awoke, drenched in sweat.

I could not get back to sleep, so I sat up thinking about the punishments I had delivered to my victims. Ferencz would deliver punishment to those who angered him, without hesitation or so much as a guilty thought. He was never incarcerated for any of his doings, in fact, he was applauded and given the name the "Dark Lord" for being such a tyrant. Margit had told me of how her former husband Jakab had punished her, yet it was accepted practice and no one ever did anything to intervene on her part. *How could men get away with such things, while a woman like me was held under lock and key? Injustice!*

My son Paul wrote to me often. It was through Paul that I learned of the everyday happenings within the empire. He was married to Judith, and they were expecting their first child. It saddened me that I missed his wedding, and that I would also miss holding another grandchild. Katalin wrote to me about her second child Erszo. Her husband György visited me, along with Paul every month. I cherished their visits, and tried not to complain of my predicament. News of my children's lives was a salve to my raw soul.

Anna had stopped writing and never visited. I asked Paul about her when he visited.

"Why doesn't Anna ever write or visit like you do, my son? All of my letters I write to her are never answered."

"Her husband hates you, Mother. I believe he was all part of this wretched conspiracy."

"He hates me? I have never given him any reason to dislike me at all. I do not understand his malevolence."

"Miklós was responsible for finding most of the evidence they say they have against you. He has been elevated in rank recently, and I doubt it is because of his military service to the crown. It is appalling the lengths he would go to in order to destroy you."

"Even though he is not on my side, would you please convey to Anna that I love her and send my good wishes to her?"

"Of course, Mother. However, I do not think that it will do much good. I believe Miklós has finally convinced her that you are a demon of sorts."

"Please do what you can and then let it be."

Months later, Paul wrote to tell me that his daughter Anna Maria had been born, and that both she and Judith were in good health. I cried over the letter as I thought about how life passed me by. I was tempted to tell Paul not to write, not to update me on anything that had happened, but I could not follow through; I wanted to know everything. Hearing from

Paul, though painful, was my only tether to reality.

When my three-year anniversary of incarceration in my chambers approached, I fell ill with excruciating stomach pains. Doubled over on my bed, I felt my stomach cramp. I was nauseated and emptied my stomach of its burning bile several times. I felt weak and feverish, and then it occurred to me that the servant had been bringing extra helpings of food. I had thought she was just being generous, but then realized that I was being poisoned.

Oh, ye gods! Why don't they just send me away to a convent in the east? Why must I be locked away in this manner? My thoughts raced. I knew little about law or how the crown courts worked. All I could do was continue to write letters to the king and to the palatine, and beg for my freedom.

Paul checked in on me and I told him of my stomach maladies.

"They're poisoning you? This is an outrage!" He reached through the slot to caress my hand, and then stormed off down the hall, and had words with the guard.

"Mother, I shall see to it that your food has not been tampered with. From now on, there will be a new cook. My guard will observe the servant as she takes a bite from your plate and swallows before serving it to you. I am also taking this directly to the king."

I was so happy that I had Paul on my side. It was like having Ferencz there as a protector the entire time. After that day, I did not have any further problems with the food. In the back of my mind, I knew that the king must have wanted to be rid of me. Thurzó would not allow my execution, so this was the king's way of going around Thurzó's stubbornness.

Days melted into nights, which melted into

immeasurable time. I was no longer frustrated by my confinement; I accepted it and simply existed. Paul and György had a small portal cut out from one of the walls so that I could peek out and see the gardens. It was thrilling to see daylight, flowers and wildlife again. Even during the winter months, I removed the tapestry which covered the opening, just to feel the intensity of the elements.

As I napped one afternoon, I was awakened by the sound of the blocks being cut away from my door. A dark figure appeared in my doorway. At first I did not recognize the person. When he removed the hood of his dark cloak, I could see that it was Thurzó.

"Countess Báthory, please rise," he asked softly.

"Have I been exonerated, my lord?"

"No, my lady."

"Then I am to finally be put to death?"

He shook his head, and fumbled underneath his cloak. He produced a large bag and handed it to me.

"Here is a bag of money, take it."

"I have no need of money. I do not understand—"

"A coach is waiting to take you wherever you wish to go, but you must leave the Kingdom of Hungary right away." He bowed his head, and waited for my response.

I was shocked. Confined for so many years, and to be set free—exiled but still free—was unfathomable.

"May I change?"

"Yes, but please hurry. You may take a few belongings with you, but you will be starting with nothing. Use the money wisely, and do stay out of trouble. I know you've been accustomed to a lavish lifestyle, but that is of the past."

"I understand," I said. In reality I was confused, but did not question him. I pulled on a comfortable kirtle and surcoat, and then brushed my hair quickly. I threw the brush into a bag, along with a few other personal items. I took with me Darvulia's Book of Shadows, some jewelry, a miniature portrait of Ferencz, and some clothes and toiletries, but nothing more. I was starting over, just as Ferencz's ghost had prophesied.

"Are you ready, my lady?"

"Yes, thank you."

"You will no longer be able to use your name, so I have prepared some papers for you. You have a new identity and a new title. Wherever you go, this should suffice to assist you in starting your new life. You are not to contact your children or step foot within the empire, for legally, Erzsébet Báthory, wife of the late Count Ferencz Nádasdy, is dead."

My face paled at the finality of it all, but I did not have to think long about my circumstances. I was free at last. He directed me out of my chambers, and we walked through the halls to the foyer. The halls seemed foreign to me. As I stepped out of my prison, I noticed that Thurzó had cleared the entire castle. The place was deserted; there were no servants bustling about cleaning or completing the daily chores of running the estate. The only other person around was the coachman, who got out of the carriage to retrieve my bag. The crisp, cold air shocked me as I stepped out of the castle.

"Here, dear cousin," Thurzó draped a cloak around my shoulders.

I did not know whether to thank the man or to spit on him. He was the bane of my existence; he had held me captive for over three miserable years, killed off my identity, and now he was releasing me back into the world with nothing. I bowed my head in acknowledgement and boarded the carriage without a word.

As we set off, I stopped the coachman and told him to wait at the base of the mountain. I watched the castle for a few moments and saw another carriage go racing up the mountainside toward the castle gates. When it stopped, I saw an auburn-haired woman being led into the castle.

I leaned out the window and called to the coachman, "Let us get going. You can take me anywhere I wish to go, is that correct?" I asked and he nodded. "Italy. I wish to go to Italy." I sat back in my seat as the coachman steered the horses down the path, away from my prison, my home, Castle Čachtice.

Author's Note

ho was Erzsébet Báthory? We know her by her popular names: The Blood Countess–Lady Dracula–The Bloody Lady of Csejte. Are these labels accurate for such a multi-faceted enigma? When someone is accused of committing such heinous crimes as Erzsébet was accused, we all want some sort of justification or reason as to why the crimes were committed. We want to give that person the benefit of the doubt, or at the very least, understand or somehow reconcile their actions, in our own minds. In Erzsébet's case, I believe we can.

In Erzsébet's time, servants were property of the aristocracy, and their master or mistress could treat them as they wanted without repercussions. A combination of her inbred ancestral roots, her naturally sadistic disposition, childhood environment, and her associates in adulthood, all likely all influenced her actions. In her naïveté and desperation to remain young and beautiful, she was easily convinced by her bloodthirsty cohorts that the fountain of youth could be found using noble blood.

As a widow, she faced many challenges politically. The Báthory-Nádasdy estates were vast and worth a fortune. King Matthias had an excellent motive for confining Erzsébet, and many good reasons not to execute her. It is possible that the documentation backing her arrest was forged or tampered with over the centuries. This may have something to do with the fact that information pertaining to the case is not easily obtained through modern political channels.

The power of misogynistic religious practices of the times, coupled with the fear of witchcraft, played a huge role in Erzsébet's condemnation. In the Middle Ages, at the very mention of the occult, people crossed themselves and prayed for protection. Their hearts and minds were led by guilt, shame and fear. The men in power were intimidated by Erzsébet, and this was a mechanism they used in their favor in order to ultimately condemn her.

There is speculation on whether or not Erzsébet really bathed in blood—that this demonic practice was used in conjunction with witchcraft. A human body contains approximately six quarts of blood, which totals around 1.5 fluid gallons. It would take the blood of several people, completely drained, to fill a tub. It is not realistic to fill a tub full of human blood and bathe in it, but it is possible to get people riled up and excited over a grandiose rumor that generates fear and astonishment.

Her alleged accomplices, who were tortured under extreme duress, would have said anything to be exonerated—it would not serve justice to believe the last words of someone being tortured—which is what most of Thurzó's case is based upon. He said that he found corpses throughout the castle. Is this really the truth? Could they have been the victims of Dorotta or Ficko alone, without Erzsébet's participation? Could they have been planted there by someone with motive to destroy Erzsébet, such as the king with help from her estranged son-in-law, Miklós Zrinyi?

Is she guilty of committing any or all of the crimes cooked up by the king's court? We may never know the whole truth, but when one thinks about all of the possibilities, it's easy to shoot holes in the prosecution's case against Erzsébet. The wild accusations, her lack of counsel and presence at any of the hearings, and the outlandish evidence that enemies claimed to dig up, amount to nothing more than a witch hunt, no different than the Salem Witch Trials of the late 17th century in America.

Aside from the accusations against Erzsébet, there are many conflicts in available data about her. Items that were not well documented include: Erzsébet's birthday; the dates of death of both of her parents, and whether or not they attended her wedding; the date of Orsolya's death, and whether or not Erzsébet lived with Orsolya before or during her marriage to Ferencz; whether or not Erzsébet had a child before she married Ferencz; specific places of burials of family members, and specific birth dates of Erzsébet's children, as well as the dates of death of the two that died.

When conducting research (especially online), one must pick through the folklore and persistent fictional glamour behind Erzsébet's story and dig through to the basic bones of factual evidence that is confirmable.

One must carefully piece together the known facts (and not be swayed by legend), question its validity and practicality, and deduce from it their own conclusions. Within this book, there are many elements that are assumed, and some that are fictional. Are they plausible? Yes. Will we ever know for sure? Probably not.

Pronunciations and English equivalents of prominent people and places within this book:

In English, Erzsébet is the equivalent of Elizabeth. Ferencz is pronounced, "FAIR-entz" and in English, is the equivalent of Francis or Franz. György is the equivalent of George in English. Sárvár is pronounced "SHAR-var". Čachtice or Csejte is pronounced "CHAHK-tee-tseh".

For further reading, check out these books:

Farin, Michael (1999). Heroine des Grauens;
ISBN 3874100383

Péter, Katalin (2001). Beloved Children: History of Aristocratic Childhood in Hungary in the Early Modern Age; ISBN 9639116777

Péter, Katalin (1985). A Csejtei Várúrnő, Bathory Erzsebet; ISBN 978-9632076522

Weston Evans, Robert John (1979, 1984).
The Making of the Habsburg Monarchy, 1550-1700: An Interpretation; ISBN 0198730853

Nagy, László (1984). A Rossz Hiru Bathoryak;
ISBN 9630923084

Keresztury, Dezso (1988). A Thousand Years of Hungarian Masterpieces; ISBN 9631325199

McNally, Raymond T. (1983). Dracula Was a Woman: In Search of the Blood Countess of Transylvania;
ISBN 0070456712

Penrose, Valentine (translated by Alexander Trocchi) (2006). The Bloody Countess: Atrocities of Erzsébet Báthory; ISBN 0971457824

On the web (current links as of 2008):

The Nádasdy Foundation
    www.nadasdy.org

The Hungarian National Museum
    www.hnm.hu

Genealogy.EU
    genealogy.euweb.cz/hung/bathori1.html
    genealogy.euweb.cz/hung/nadasdy2.html

The Ferencz Nádasdy Museum of Hungary
    www.museum.hu/sarvar/nadasdy

A. Mordeaux
    www.mordeaux.com

Made in the USA
Lexington, KY
28 February 2015